HALF MY FACEBOOK
FRIENDS ARE FERRETS

Half My Facebook Friends Are Ferrets is published in the United States by
Switch Press
A Capstone Imprint
1710 Roe Crest Drive
North Mankato, Minnesota 56003
www.switchpress.com

First published in 2014 by Curious Fox,
an imprint of Capstone Global Library Limited,
7 Pilgrim Street, London, EC4V 6LB
Registered company number: 6695582
www.curious-fox.com

Library of Congress Cataloging-in-Publication Data is available
on the Library of Congress website.

ISBN: 978-1-63079-000-4 (paper over board)
ISBN: 978-1-63079-011-0 (ebook)

Summary: Sixteen-year-old Josh has a lot he wants to accomplish before he
turns seventeen. As it stands, he's a wannabe metalhead, he's never been
kissed, and he's nowhere near as cool as people say his dad was.

Cover Image Credits - Shutterstock: Eric Isselee (ferret), Vladimir Gorokhov
(mohawk)

Printed in China.
032014   008081RRDF14

TO SOPHIE AND JASMINE,
FOR BEING INSPIRATIONAL

MONDAY, JANUARY 6TH —
6 MONTHS TILL MY 17TH BIRTHDAY

10:20 A.M.: LOWER DUNGEON
(A.K.A. ENGLISH HALLWAY)

Today I have to do a presentation at school. It counts toward my final English grade, so I feel like I should make an effort. Mrs. Barber, our English teacher, refuses to say just how much it counts. This makes me kind of suspicious. I wouldn't be surprised if it's less than half a percent.

At least my presentation will be interesting. So far we have had to sit through "Nail Art Through the Ages," "Lady Gaga: Style Queen," and "Eating for a Healthy Complexion." I'm still wondering if I made the right choice, though. I had three ideas originally:

1. **"Ferrets: Their Role in Modern Society"**

2. **"The Major Pentatonic Scale and Its Use in Improvising Riffs"**

3. **"The Satanic Roots of Death Metal"**

I decided to go with the last one, feeling it had the edge excitement-wise, but now I wonder if it might be a little too exciting, especially for Mrs. Barber, who's coming up on retirement age and rumored to have heart trouble.

"Who is up next?" says Mrs. Barber, consulting her list. "Ah yes, Joshua. Come on up, dear."

Mrs. Barber summons me to the front of the room, and I suddenly notice the St. Christopher pendant hanging around her neck. My PowerPoint has pictures of church burnings!

To calm my nerves, I take a few deep breaths and remember Ollie's advice to imagine everyone in the room naked.

Unfortunately, Charlotte Anderson is in the front row, and imagining her naked sets off a stirring below. This would be fine if my jeans weren't so tight, but Mom refuses to buy new ones due to our "financial difficulties."

"Do you have a PowerPoint?" Mrs. Barber asks.

"Oh! Oh yes, um. Yes, I do," I admit.

"Excellent," she says. "Some nice slides for us to look at."

"Um . . . sort of . . . not really."

Mrs. Barber looks uncertain. "What exactly is your presentation on, dear?"

2:45 P.M.: HALFWAY DOWN SOME
STREET OR OTHER

"Fantastic presentation," says Ollie on the way home. "Especially that part where you showed the slide of the

6

demon with three buttholes and Mrs. Barber had the panic attack."

"Thank you, Ollie," I say. "Damn! I knew I should've done the one on ferrets."

"Don't worry," Ollie goes on. "Mrs. Barber will be okay; a quick visit to the hospital will probably do her good."

I say goodbye to Ollie at the corner by his house and wander home. Thankfully, no one is there to ask how the nightmare presentation went.

I go to my bedroom, say hi to Ozzy, my ferret, and reach under the bed for the giant leather-bound notebook Mom gave me. Yeah, I know — some teenagers get PlayStations for Christmas. I get a notebook.

When she gave it to me, Mom tried to talk up the present by saying, "It has two hundred pages of extra high quality paper!"

"Amazing," I said.

"So you can write on both sides without the ink showing through."

"Awesome, Mom. Really awesome."

"But the important thing," she droned on, "is that this can be your release valve, Josh. When I was young, I wrote down all the bad things that happened to me in a journal like this, and I felt much better. It helped me get out all of my angry, destructive feelings."

Maybe you should write in one again then, I thought, but I just nodded and put the book with my other gifts (a festive package of Ghirardelli chocolates and an assortment of scented gel pens).

I'm wondering if I should use the notebook for its intended purpose. I do need a release valve one way or another.

I open the journal and make a list of things that are bad in my life. It's not complete — that would take hours. But it's a start.

Things that are bad in my life:

1. I am 16½ and have never been kissed . . . unless you count Nana, Mom, Mrs. Stokes, Aunt Sarah, Ollie's Labrador Bongo, and my cousin Anna. And Bongo's kiss was more of a slurp.

2. I look nerdy and I don't even wear glasses.

3. We have "financial difficulties."

4. My mother is the strictest parent on the planet.

5. Girls think I'm a dick . . .

Good. Excellent. Do I feel any better?

No.

TUESDAY, JANUARY 7TH

12:10 P.M.: SOCCER FIELD WITH PETER, DAVEY, AND OLLIE

"Looking at me," I say, "would you say I come across as, oh . . . nerdy?"

"Nah," says Ollie. "You're too stupid to be nerdy."

"Thanks," I say. "But I mean . . . if you didn't know that?"

"I'd say you're more of a geek," says Davey.

"A geek! Davey, if anyone is a geek it's you."

"Uh, I may be a lot of things, but I am not a geek."

"You kind of are," I say.

"Just because I wear glasses . . ."

"What about your periodic table mug?" I remind him.

"That was a gift."

"The *Jeopardy* quiz books?"

"I was going through a phase."

"The *Apollo 13* space module poster on your door?"

Davey holds up his hands. "Okay, you got me."

"Well," says Ollie, "I don't think being nerdy's so bad anyway. I saw a girl in the mall once with a sweatshirt that said 'I love nerds' on it. At least I think that's what it said. It wasn't easy to make out because of her enormous boobs."

"Right," I say.

"The words were kinda stretched."

"Yeah, Ollie, we get it."

"Well, all I know," says Peter, "is that whatever you are, you should be proud."

"Jesus, Peter," Ollie says. "That is so gay."

"I know," says Peter happily, since he's almost certainly gay.

WEDNESDAY, JANUARY 8TH

4:45 P.M.: INNER SANCTUM (A.K.A. BEDROOM)

School seemed to go on forever today. But when I empty out my backpack, I discover it's still not over, because I now have a mountain of math homework to do! Mr. Cain, our teacher, obviously thinks none of us have anything better to do than slave over decimals all evening. In my case, he could be right . . . but how would he know that?

5:20 P.M.

The home phone rings, and I rush downstairs. It's Davey. Why he can't text like normal kids is beyond me.

"Have you done your math yet?" he says.

"Some of it," I say.

"I don't get it."

"What don't you get?"

"Anything!"

Davey sounds desperate, but I'm used to this. He knows how to turn on the emotional blackmail. But while it works with his mom, it won't work with me.

"Well, maybe you should ask Mr. Cain," I say.

"Huh?"

"Mr. Cain, our math teacher."

"But then he'll realize I'm dumb and move me down a level. And I won't survive ten minutes with the morons, Josh!"

I can hear Davey's breathing through the phone, short and rapid, like he has just climbed Mount Everest, or in Davey's case, walked down his hallway.

"Calm down, Davey," I say. "Let's go through it slowly. Now what you need to do —"

"Can't you just tell me the answers?" he asks.

"What?"

"*Iron Man 3* is streaming online."

5:30 P.M.: BACK IN INNER SANCTUM

I'm a softie — that's the problem. Even Ozzy takes advantage of my wonderful nature. Currently he is rolling around in my clean laundry, shedding an asthmatic's nightmare of black and white hairs. I'm getting the occasional whiff of ferret food too. Thanks, Ozzy. I'm really gonna attract the opposite sex with my jeans smelling like liver!

THURSDAY, JANUARY 9TH

1:15 P.M.: LA BASTILLE (A.K.A. FRENCH)

Madame Zizi, our French teacher, just told us to write a paragraph about our family, but since I don't know the French for "ridiculously bad-tempered psychos," it's gonna be difficult for me. Madame Zizi says we can finish our paragraph at home.

Does one sentence count as a paragraph?

Absolutely it does, which means I can spend the entire evening chilling out to Megadeth and designing a cool cover for my album. Yes!!

Looking at me, you would never guess I'm a metalhead. I look like I'd be more into Cher or the local over-eighties male glee club than Morbid Angel or Slayer. This is because my mom insists that my hair is kept short and in the least fashionable style known to man. She also believes that wearing black T-shirts is satanic. My mother is the most repressed, nun-like person I know. How she ever had kids is beyond me.

6:00 P.M.: KITCHEN

Currently Mother Superior is out tending to the needs of the various old folks she looks after, so I make myself a delicious dinner of cornflakes and smoky bacon chips.

I am just finishing up and am debating whether

it's a bad idea to eat four bowls of cornflakes in a row when Mom and my sister come in. My sister kicks off her stilettos and collapses in the chair opposite me. She looks like she had a fight with a blow-dryer, but I don't want to die a virgin, so I decide not to mention this.

"Good day at work, Maddie?" I say.

"F*** off," she replies.

I have an on/off relationship with my sister.

Mostly off.

Mom is shifting things around in the fridge. "Don't tell me someone used up all the milk," she mutters.

"Not me," I say, moving my math textbook in front of my cereal bowl.

"Our neighbor Mrs. Hughes has a fridge that warns you when you're running out of milk," says Maddie.

"Does she now," says Mom.

"She got it as part of that ten-grand renovation on her kitchen."

I try to give Mom a sympathetic look, but she has turned around to put a pot of water on to boil.

Sadly, it'd take ten grand to bring our house up to squatter's standards. Not that it's dirty or anything . . . it's just caught in a '70s time warp. We could make money by opening it as a museum. "And here you see vintage 1970s wallpaper. Note the globular pattern in shades of burnt umber. Barf bags can be found to your right."

Also, a lot of things don't work. I've given up eating fish sticks due to the three-foot-high drifts of snow in our freezer, and the last time I tried using the oven I was almost incinerated.

Mom says this is what happens when you don't have a man around. Which is kind of hurtful considering I'm almost seventeen and definitely of the male persuasion, but I know what she means.

We don't have Dad, is what she means.

SATURDAY, JANUARY 11TH

10:45 A.M.: INNER SANCTUM

Today is an Ozzy cleaning day. As I get out his towel and the ferret shampoo, Ozzy eyes me suspiciously through his black bandit mask. He does not like being washed.

11:10 A.M.

Hmm, the bathroom looks like it's been hit by a tsunami. My clothes are soaking wet. I have several large scratches on the insides of my arms, and a bruise is forming where I smacked my head on the sink.

Ozzy is very clean though! He is also very annoyed.

3:30 P.M.: MR. PITMAN'S HOUSE

I am young, I'm not suffering from any serious health issues, and I am a "drain on resources," which in Mom's opinion means I should be working.

Never mind that I have homework. Never mind that I need to wash Ozzy, update my Facebook account, and spy on other people's accounts to find out what amazing stuff they're up to so that I can feel really jealous.

This is not enough for my mom. If she had her way, I'd be digging up turnips in the snow at 5:00 a.m.

But in fact she has me doing something worse — entertaining Mr. Pitman.

Mr. Pitman lives down the street from us and suffers from arthritis. When it's bad, he can hardly bend over to put his socks on. Ever since his wife left last year, Mom has been cleaning and shopping for him. And since Mom is great at guilt-tripping me into doing anything she wants, I walk his dog (a yappy Yorkshire terrier). I also mow his lawn and play chess with him or, on very depressing days, Parcheesi.

Mr. Pitman always wins, because try as I might, I cannot get into a game of Parcheesi. Maybe if it was strip Parcheesi with Megan Fox . . . anyway, where was I? Oh yes, moving my little green game piece.

Mr. Pitman tosses the dice with vigor, causing them to spring off the board and land in Minty's bed (Minty is the dog).

"Whoops, sorry," says Mr. Pitman as I delve into Minty's hair-encrusted blankets.

"Grrr," says Minty.

"She won't hurt you," says Mr. Pitman. "She's just a little thing."

Yes, but her teeth are like hypodermic needles, I feel like saying.

Minty seems to remember that I'm her ticket out of this hellhole, so she resists savaging my face.

"Your turn," says Mr. Pitman.

It's the weekend, and I should be getting into all sorts of teenage shenanigans. Instead I'm sitting here feeling my brain about to implode due to lack of use. I roll a two.

"Unlucky," says Mr. Pitman.

MONDAY, JANUARY 13TH

9:35 A.M.: TOWER OF TERROR
(A.K.A. MATH HALLWAY)

Mr. Pitman's house is depressing, but it has nothing on school. If one more person tells me, "Cheer up, son. These are the best days of your life!" I might have to pin them down, attach electrodes to their private parts, and send several thousand volts of electricity coursing through their bodies.

These are certainly NOT the best days of my life. At least, I damn well hope not!

Today in geometry, for example, Mr. Cain informs me that he had to give me an F for my homework because the handwriting was so bad. "You are sixteen, Joshua," he says. "You should be able to write."

I say, "You are fifty, Mr. Cain. You should be able to read!"

Actually, I just nod and promise to write it out again.

10:45 A.M.: FIELD OF NIGHTMARES (A.K.A. ATHLETIC FIELD)

And now in PE, Lydia Smart just came over and said to me, "There's a party at Hannah Harrigan's on Saturday. Don't bother coming, you're not invited."

What was the point of that? She just walked right across the field to tell me that.

There are girls in this school who are downright nasty. They make Simon Cowell look like Gandhi.

Not that I'd want to go to Hannah Harrigan's party anyway. Her dad is some big shot in the local police department. He'd probably arrest you for dropping a tortilla chip.

Davey comes and stands beside me, and we watch

the two teams slog up one end of the field, miss the goal, and slog back again. No one seems very enthusiastic about the lacrosse game aside from Mr. Cox, the PE teacher. People must be able to hear him shouting in France.

Davey wipes his nose on the bottom of his PE shirt and says, "Did Hannah invite you to her party?"

"No," I say. "She invited me not to. Or actually her brainless buddy Lydia did."

"Me too," says Davey.

I look at Davey shivering in his XXL T-shirt. "Cheer up," I say. "Girls' parties are lame anyway."

"How do you know?"

"Well, I don't know for sure. But they have to be. I mean all they do is giggle and give each other manicures."

"Yeah, but there'll be boys there," says Davey. "Most of the boys in our class are going."

"Really?" I say.

Mr. Cox is waving us onto the field. "Get a move on, you lazy slackers!" he yells. If you closed your eyes, you could imagine you were in Basic Training in the deserts of Afghanistan. Except for the freezing rain, mud, and extreme cold, that is.

I notice that Lydia has been chosen to face off, which is pretty appropriate. I am determined to whack her hard in the ankles at least twice before the game is over. I might even aim higher.

5:45 P.M.: INNER SANCTUM

I am home late because I had to stay after school and shovel slush off the track. I am definitely off Mr. Cox's Christmas list. He has a bruise the size of Jupiter on his shin. How was I supposed to know he'd dive in the way just as I was about to clobber Lydia? It's his fault for being so enthusiastic.

TUESDAY, JANUARY 14TH

5:00 P.M.: INNER SANCTUM, WRITING IN MY LEATHER-BOUND NOTEBOOK

> *Got no respect for Lydia Smart*
> *Girls like her can't touch my heart*
> *If I had to choose between her or death*
> *I'd dig my grave and hold my breath*
>
> **From the album: *No Respect for***
> ***Lydia Smart,* by Joshua Walker**

Okay, so I'm terrible at looking cool, attracting women, and getting invited places. But on the bright side, I'm awesome at guitar!

The only problem is that due to "financial difficulties," I can't have a Randy Rhoads Flying V Jackson with blue ghost flames, an ebony fingerboard, and mother-of-pearl shark fin inlays ($799.95, Steve's Music Emporium). In fact, I can't have an electric guitar at all.

Mr. Trumper, the music teacher at school, told me that my acoustic will give me a great start, but what he doesn't realize is that my acoustic is a child's, three-quarter size, nylon-string classical.

It's great for "Greensleeves," terrible for "Highway to Hell."

Anyway, I play some of the classical masterpiece "Spanish Romance," which I can do pretty well, and am just about to consult my Vladimir Axegrinder *Death Metal for Dummies* book, when Ozzy scampers over and starts jumping around and gnawing on the cover.

Ozzy has no respect. Vladimir is an icon in the death metal guitar world.

The doorbell rings, and I go downstairs. Davey is standing on the porch, and he has a reddish hue. Combined with his short hair and round face, he looks like a worried beet.

"I hate girls," he says.

I nod, thinking that maybe Lydia or Hannah has made some cruel remark about his huge nose, festering zits, or terrible hairstyle.

Davey pokes my chest. "Aren't you gonna ask me to come inside?" he says.

"Sorry," I say. "Come on up."

When we get upstairs, Davey collapses heavily on my bed, which worries me, because if the legs break, I'll be sleeping on the floor for the next ten years.

"I wish I was twelve," he says.

I raise my eyebrows.

"I hate being a teenager."

"Ah . . ."

"I hate having these . . . you know . . . urges . . ."

I know where Davey's coming from here. One of the worst things about being a teenager is that girls (some of them at least) start to look attractive.

I preferred it when they were annoying little wannabe princesses running around with ice cream dripping down their chins and Barbie dolls in their underwear. (This refers to my cousin Anna, who is seriously weird and probably not representative of most little girls.)

"My mom will never speak to me again," Davey continues.

"What happened, Davey?"

"She will never forgive me . . ."

"Davey! What happened?"

What happened was Davey had decided to deal with his urges by taking matters into his own hands . . .

literally. He lay down on his bed, closed his eyes, put some music on his headphones, and . . . well . . . got busy.

Anyway, a short time later he thought, *Hey, what I could go for right now is a nice hot drink.* He opened his eyes and right there on his nightstand was a steaming mug of hot chocolate!

"Are you sure it wasn't there before?" I ask him. "Maybe you forgot you made it."

"I didn't forget."

"Your mind was on other things," I remind him.

"Josh, either I have developed amazing telepathic powers or . . . my mom brought it in a few minutes earlier."

"Oh," I say. "Eeew!"

"Thanks!"

I sympathize with Davey, but at least his mom understands about men and their urges.

My mom understands nothing. If she burst in on me doing that, she'd send me off to some Tibetan monastery to get castrated or beheaded or something.

If Dad was around it would be easier, but Dad will never be around. My dad died when I was a baby. He worked as a driller on an oil rig in the Gulf. Strangely, he didn't die in some horrific drilling accident but from a plain old heart attack. Turns out he had a congenital heart defect that no one knew about. Luckily, my sister and I don't have it — or so Mom says. Anyway, Dad was only thirty-one when he died, so he will always look young, cool, and super-strong like he does in his photo in the hallway.

I send Davey on his way with the mantra "it could've been worse." It could have been his grandma who came in with the hot chocolate. She might have thought he was having a seizure and called 911 for an ambulance. I think that made Davey feel better.

WEDNESDAY, JANUARY 15TH

10:10 P.M.: INNER SANCTUM

I take out my leather-bound notebook and rip out the page about things that are bad in my life. Who needs that kind of negativity?

Instead, the same way people write lists of places they should see before they die, I am writing a list of things I should do before I'm seventeen. Currently they are:

1. Be kissed by someone who is female, but not a relative, very old, very young, or covered in fur (i.e., get a girlfriend!).

2. Master the famous "One" by Metallica.

3. See Children of Bodom live. (I might have to travel to Finland for this, but

that's a small price to pay — at least metaphorically.)

4. Be the proud owner of a Randy Rhoads Flying V Jackson with blue ghost flames, ebony fingerboard, and mother-of-pearl shark fin inlays.

5. Get something pierced or tattooed!

6. Be half as cool as people say my dad was.

The easiest (or least impossible) of these is probably number 2, so I go and print out the music for "One" from the computer. It is over nine pages long! Luckily, I won't be seventeen for another five and a half months.

FRIDAY, JANUARY 17TH

4:15 P.M.: PASSAGE TO FORBIDDING GATEWAY (A.K.A. FRONT HALLWAY)

Great, a letter for me! I hardly ever get letters.

I rip open the envelope and find that I have qualified for a 50-percent reduction on the cost of an AmeriGlide stair lift.

WTF?

1:10 P.M.: KITCHEN

I am sitting eating lunch (a family-size bag of smoky bacon chips) and enjoying a fantastic metal-stardom daydream in which I am being suffocated by hordes of adoring, insanely attractive female fans, when who should come in but my sister and her crappy boyfriend, Clint.

I mean . . . Clint? What kind of name is that? It sounds more like a furniture polish than a person.

"What's up, bro," says Clint, thumping me hard on the back. "Got yourself a girlfriend yet?"

"Don't tease him," says Maddie as she looks through the fridge.

"I ain't teasing; good-lookin' guy like him should be fighting 'em off with a stick."

"I don't have time for a girlfriend," I tell him. "I'm concentrating on my schoolwork." Unlike some idiots I could mention who wouldn't know a quadratic equation if it came up and bit him in the nuts.

"Lot of good that'll do ya," says Clint. "Look at me — not one good grade to my name, and I did all right."

"You're unemployed," I remind him.

Clint leans over and slams both fists on the table. He really is gigantic; his arms are wider than most people's bodies.

"That's 'cause there's no jobs!" he roars. "You think I wanna be outta work?"

"Clint, babe, leave him alone," says my sister. "He didn't mean it."

"Yes, well, I'm going on Facebook," I say, getting up from the table.

"Oh yeah." Clint laughs. "Bet you got tons of friends, huh?"

"Quite a few," I say.

"Too bad most of 'em are ferrets!"

Even my traitor of a sister laughs at this.

I leave the room without replying.

How dare he. Less than half of my Facebook friends are ferrets.

MONDAY, JANUARY 20TH

5:50 P.M.: KITCHEN
(MOTHER SUPERIOR NOT YET HOME)

My sister bought me a bottle of beer today, probably as a peace offering. I hide it in my closet so Mom can't find it. Mom says alcohol causes nothing but pain and torment, but God knows why she thinks that. My life is full of pain and torment, and I've hardly had any alcohol.

Anyway, if Maddie thinks she can buy my forgiveness with beer she's . . . probably right.

TUESDAY, JANUARY 21ST

8:00 P.M.: INNER SANCTUM

I've decided that in order to be cool like my dad (number six on my list), I need to build up some muscles. Needless to say, we don't have any suitable weight-training equipment, so I have to use whatever I can find. In this case, a large bottle of soda (three-quarters drunk) and Ozzy.

At first, Ozzy likes being lifted up and down. He makes excited dooking noises and stares at all the cobwebs on the walls, but then he gets scared and lets out a fart. An eye-wateringly bad one! Jeez, I bet Dad didn't have to put up with farting ferrets when he was weight lifting.

WEDNESDAY, JANUARY 22ND

11:00 P.M.: INNER SANCTUM, LISTENING TO CHILDREN OF BODOM ON MY HEADPHONES

I wonder how much it costs to go to Finland . . .

THURSDAY, JANUARY 23RD

6:30 P.M.: KITCHEN WITH MOTHER SUPERIOR

"Finland!" announces my mom. "Listen to me, Josh.

If I can ever afford to go on a vacation, which seems unlikely given our 'financial difficulties,' then I certainly won't be going to some godforsaken place where it snows nine-tenths of the year and barely sees daylight. I will go to Corfu."

I feel like I should point out the huge geographical and meteorological inaccuracies in this statement, but I can't be bothered. My mother has no soul.

It's no good telling her that Finland is the coolest place on the planet. That there are twenty-five hundred metal bands there, which in a country with a population of five million, means that every two-hundredth person is in a band. I mean, if you had to come up with a statistic for where I live, it'd probably be that every two-hundredth person has a walker!

"Finland," says my mom again. She has the nerve to pat me on the head and chuckle as I open the front door to leave.

I say, "For f***'s sake, Mom, you are about as adventurous as an egg salad sandwich!"

Actually, I say, "Bye. Peter's mom is bringing me home."

7:00 P.M.: RANGERS AT THE LOCAL PARK

People think Rangers is for little kids, but I go to Ranger Teens, which is for fourteen- to seventeen-year-olds. True, it's not an activity you'd usually associate with metal, but a few girls go, and there's always a chance that one of them might help me out with my sheepshanks!

Tonight we are doing trust exercises in the Visitor's Center. I'm excited because there is potential for bodily contact, but suddenly I notice that none of the girls are here today. Great! Now, I'm facing bodily contact with a bunch of sweaty, zit-infested boys. If that's what I was looking for, I should've stayed home alone in bed.

In the first activity, we have to form a circle while a blindfolded Ranger stands in the center, arms folded over his chest. The "victim" then leans forward and is caught by one of us and pushed back to the middle.

One thing's for sure: I definitely don't want to be the person in the center. Not because I'm scared, but because I'm five foot eleven — about three feet taller than everyone else. When they see me looming toward them they'll scatter like dropped peas!

Shaun, our leader, will realize this, though, and pick one of the smaller ones.

"Josh, in the middle please," Shaun says.

"But . . ."

A bunch of chicken impersonators suddenly fill the room, so I am forced to accept my fate. My nose is just about my only decent feature, but soon it'll be a busted-up wreck.

"Good luck," says a husky female voice.

I turn and come face to face with the most beautiful girl I've ever seen. Well, maybe not the most beautiful. I mean, there are better-looking people in movies and maybe even in Target, but she is pretty hot. Also, she seems to be kind of a rock chick.

I am just trying to figure out if the thing on her nose is a stud or a booger when Shaun yanks the blindfold down over my head and pushes me into the center.

5 MINUTES LATER

Well, the past five minutes were some of the scariest of my life. My nose remained intact, but my bladder almost didn't. I'm feeling pretty relieved when I remove the blindfold and take my place back in the circle.

"Hmm," says Shaun. "You were kind of rough with Joshua. Sure, he's a big guy and can take it, but I want things to be a lot less manic this time."

Thanks, Shaun. Nice of you to show your concern.

"Now as some of you might have noticed, we have a new recruit tonight," Shaun goes on. "Would you like to go in the middle, Charlene?"

I can see now that Charlene has a nose stud. And a Pantera tattoo. I can't believe it. A girl into metal, and I am just about to catch her in my arms!

Charlene is moved around the circle very gently. Some

of the boys look panic-stricken as she leans their way. In typical fashion, she is not pushed toward me once. Oh well, it looks like we are moving on to something else now.

"So, as you see, we have some benches and buckets laid out," says Shaun, waving around the room. "I want you to choose a partner and lead them, blindfolded, around the course."

I feel awful; my friend Peter, who I've known since before I was born (our moms were in prenatal classes together), starts making his way over, but Charlene has already come over and is standing beside me! Out of the corner of my eye, I see Peter's rejected look. Now he will have to be paired with someone by Shaun, or even worse, be partnered with Shaun himself. The embarrassment will be crushing. Still, it can't be helped . . .

"So, you're Josh," Charlene says.

"Certainly am," I say. "Yep, that's me all right . . . uh, I can't help noticing you're into metal," I go on quickly.

"Def," she says, giving me the metal salute. "I've seen tons of bands."

"Awesome," I say.

"Slayer, Metallica, Napalm Death. And I've been to Orion."

"Orion?"

"You know, the famous touring metal festival."

"Oh, that Orion," I say.

Charlene puts on her blindfold and grabs my arm. "You should go to it with your friends."

"Yeah, totally," I say. I don't tell her that Davey is into modern jazz, Ollie, R&B, and Peter, Broadway.

While we're navigating the benches, I ruffle my neckerchief a little and untuck my shirt to try to hide the fact that my Ranger pants go up to my armpits.

"Josh, you're really a mess today!" yells Shaun from the other side of the room. "You won't impress our new recruit with your shirt all untucked."

I sigh dramatically.

"And what is up with your woggle?" he shouts, looking scornfully at the fastener holding my neckerchief in place. "Straighten it, please."

Charlene takes off the blindfold and gives me a grin. "He's kind of fussy, isn't he?"

"Yeah," I say. "Fascist pig!"

Luckily, Shaun doesn't hear this or I'd be kicked out of Rangers for good.

9:35 P.M.

"Will you be here next week?" Shaun asks Charlene as she puts on her coat.

"I'm not sure," she says. "I think I might be dyeing my hair."

9:40 P.M.

"Well, nice girl, but somehow I don't think it was her thing," says Shaun once Charlene has left and just Peter and I are left waiting to get picked up.

"It was Josh's fault," Peter says. "He scared her off with his wonky woggle."

FRIDAY, JANUARY 24TH

7:30 P.M.: DEN, ON INTERNET

I spend about an hour on our crappy secondhand computer trying to find Charlene on Facebook. You'd think with a name like that it would be easy, but the only possible Charlene lives in Nome, Alaska, which is a little too far to come for Rangers.

I'm starting to wonder if she made up that name to sound cool. Her real name is probably Mavis Block or something. I start typing Mavis Block into Facebook's search box but then realize I'm being seriously crazy. Oh well, number 1 on my list will have to wait a little longer. I must let Charlene go and move on.

SATURDAY, JANUARY 25TH

2:30 P.M.: LIVING ROOM

Mom says that one of her "people" (as she calls the folks she makes a living cleaning, cooking, and shopping for) knows someone who knows someone who used to work in that diner behind the grocery store called the Dead Duck and that they could get me a job there — maybe. Would I like that?

"Yes," I say. "I'd love to work in a divey, late-night diner that's called the Dead Duck and is full of pathetic, lonely drunks." It's not really called the Dead Duck, but it's something like that.

Mom gets annoyed and mentions "financial difficulties" about sixty million times.

I say, "Oh, all right."

She smiles and leaves. Damn her.

MONDAY, JANUARY 27TH

7:00 P.M.: INNER SANCTUM, DOING HOMEWORK

The problem with being sixteen — or one of them — is that there are so many decisions to make. Right now, I'm wondering if I should have taken world history instead of earth science.

Rivers or Russians?

Hot spots or Hitler?

Well, it's too late now.

World history sounds damn easy though. At lunch

today, Ollie said his teacher told him that World War I started because of a sandwich. Apparently, after this Serbian terrorist failed to assassinate Franz Ferdinand (the Archduke, not the band), he went to a café for a quick snack. Then, just as he came out, Franz happened to be there after making a wrong turn in his car. The Serbian grabbed his gun and immediately shot Franz in the neck.

I tried to respond with a similarly interesting story about sedimentary rocks, but none came to mind.

WEDNESDAY, JANUARY 29TH

I receive a pair of extra-large control-top tights in the mail.

Why?

THURSDAY, JANUARY 30TH

7:50 P.M.: RANGERS

I give Peter my control-top tights and am surprised by how offended he gets.

He says, "Just because I'm almost certainly gay doesn't mean I want to dress up in women's tights. Besides, I'm a small."

He doesn't give them back, though.

7:20 P.M.: INNER SANCTUM

Ozzy is investigating my English Lit. book, *To Kill a Mockingbird.* Most ferrets probably would kill a mockingbird if given half a chance, but Ozzy is about as aggressive as a heart-shaped candy.

A door bangs somewhere, and Ozzy jumps and pees a little on page ten. I feel like I should apologize to Harper Lee, but she's a multimillionaire, so I don't.

Anyway, it's Saturday evening, and I'm stuck here writing an essay for my English homework. How sad is that? After a half hour, I've still only written forty-eight words, and twenty of those are the question.

Ozzy starts dancing and hopping around on my desk, which isn't helping. I try to nudge him off, but he thinks I'm fooling around and he runs off with my pen. Can't he tell that I'm not in the mood for games? That I'm slowly dying inside?

> *Like a mockingbird*
> *Whose song is unheard*
> *Whose beak has been tied*
> *Slowly dying inside*
>
> **From the album: *Slowly Dying Inside,* by Josh Walker**

SUNDAY, FEBRUARY 2ND

2:00 P.M.: INNER SANCTUM

Crappy day today. I broke a string on my guitar, so I can't practice, which is seriously annoying since I still have another eight and three-quarter pages of Metallica's "One" to get through.

MONDAY, FEBRUARY 3RD

6:15 P.M.: INNER SANCTUM

Another crappy day! Mrs. Barber said that "my ferret stole my pen" was not a good enough excuse for failing to hand in my *Mockingbird* homework, so she gave me detention.

Then, after I got home, Mom had a hardcore rant at me just for being in her room.

"I don't want you poking around," she said. "I have certain things in there that are . . . private."

Honestly, all I wanted was some of that perfume she uses on special occasions. Ozzy had a little accident on the carpet, and I wanted to cover up the smell. That's what I get for trying to keep things clean and hygienic around here!

Anyway, I have a French test tomorrow, so I'd better start studying.

TUESDAY, FEBRUARY 4TH —
5 MONTHS TILL MY 17TH BIRTHDAY

10:15 A.M.: LA BASTILLE (FRENCH ORAL EXAM)

"When you're ready," says Madame Zizi.

I stutter off the paragraph I've memorized about my hobbies, friends, and family. Luckily, the English and French words for guitar are more or less the same, so that's at least one word I got right.

Throughout my speech, Madame Zizi grimaces and pulls at her hair.

Probably not a very good sign.

THURSDAY, FEBRUARY 6TH

7:30 P.M.: DEN

Rangers has been canceled tonight, because Shaun injured his thumb demonstrating knots and lashings to the Tuesday group.

I decide to quickly log onto Facebook in case any ravishing girls have sent me a friend request. Or maybe even a girlfriend request.

Nope, no friend requests. But I do have four *FantasticFarm* requests from Ollie to harvest his crops, rake his leaves, water his onions, and build some new stables.

I have three *PurrfectPets* requests from Davey to pamper his puppies, feed his parrot, and stroke his rabbits.

And I have two *MasterDinerChef* requests from Peter to clean the toilets and make two dozen cupcakes with frosting before 9:00 p.m.

9:45 P.M.

I log off of Facebook feeling exhausted. I might have to delete my account if this continues.

FRIDAY, FEBRUARY 7TH

8:00 P.M.: INNER SANCTUM

Mom comes in (without knocking) and tells me I have an interview at the Deceased Duck tomorrow. "Isn't that exciting?" she says.

"Extremely," I answer.

Mom smiles and leaves. Sarcasm is lost on her.

8:10 P.M.

Hold on, though. If Mom lets me keep my pay, I might actually be able to afford the wondrous Jackson Flying V . . . thereby achieving number 4 on my list. Now *that* is exciting!

7:00 P.M.: LOCAL DIVEY DINER

Yay! I have been hired as an employee at the Duck Revived. My job isn't very demanding brain-wise, but it does mean I have super-clean hands. Yep, I am a dishwasher.

Anyway, Mom'll be happy. From now on she'll probably only mention "financial difficulties" every half hour or so. But even better — a minor miracle has occurred. She said I can keep what I earn. All of it!

Mrs. Barnes, the owner, introduces me to the chef, Derek. Derek smiles and extends a friendly hand, and I notice his nails are kind of dirty and there are a few warts on his fingers. I make a mental note to never eat anything from the Duck Revived but to heartily recommend its culinary delights to Mr. Cain, my math teacher.

"And this is Michelle," says Mrs. Barnes, grabbing the arm of a passing angel. "Michelle is our waitress. She's very popular with the clientele."

Looking at Michelle's perfect figure and model-like features, I can see why. She is definitely potential girlfriend material.

"This is Joshua," Mrs. Barnes says. "He's going to be helping out every Saturday, washing the dishes and putting out the garbage."

Great introduction, Mrs. Barnes. Thanks for that.

Michelle looks at me briefly (i.e., the way all girls look at me) before disappearing back into the diner.

Michelle, ma belle . . . I hum to myself. Jeez! I make another mental note to bring headphones next week so I don't start corrupting my musical tastes by randomly singing old Beatles songs. Or even worse, country and bluegrass music, which seem to be playing at the Duck 24/7.

Mrs. Barnes hands me an apron before droning on a while longer. Allegedly, if I prove reliable in the plate-cleaning department, I can advance to more sophisticated tasks such as taking people's orders and assembling salad garnishes! The anticipation is almost too much for me.

7:30 P.M.: SINK

Jesus, "Stand by Your Man" is a very catchy song. If I sing it one more time, I might have to stick an unwashed fork in my eye. Music like that should come with a health warning.

"WARNING: This crap is weirdly addictive. It might seriously damage your brain and could make you want to take up lassoing as a hobby."

Mrs. Barnes suddenly swoops in from the dining room to inspect my handiwork. "Did you rinse these?" she asks, pointing at the stack of plates.

"Absolutely," I say.

She runs a finger across one, and I feel strangely anxious. I try to read her expression, but she's giving nothing away. After an uncomfortable few seconds, she nods and says, "Carry on."

"Thanks," I gush. "Thanks very much!"

God, what is wrong with me? Why do I give a dry roasted peanut what Mrs. Barnes thinks?

I am starved for affection — that's what it is.

I desperately need a girlfriend! Michelle, do you know how happy I'd be if you were just to make eye contact? Just acknowledging my existence would make me delirious with pleasure.

Michelle appears and dumps a pile of gravy-soaked plates on the draining board. It'll have to do for now.

10:45 P.M.

Finally, I can leave. Mrs. Barnes passes me some greasy five-dollar bills. She looks sneaky, and I realize this is what people mean when they talk about paying "under the table." I nod back in a similarly sneaky way and go outside to check how much I've made.

Twenty dollars. Twenty measly dollars! At this rate, I'll never be able to afford the wondrous Jackson.

Of course, I could always ask for some more shifts. About a million more!

Or . . . here's a thought: I could sell my body! It's not much, but it's gotta be worth a few dollars to someone. If they didn't want it for sex, I could sell them a lung or something. Do people sell lungs?

SUNDAY, FEBRUARY 9TH

9:45 A.M.: KITCHEN

Mom gave me an old pickle jar to put my savings in, and I just made a label for it:

JACKSON GUITAR FUND

Not to be touched under pain of death! Seriously!!

I am just about to stick it on the jar when Mom asks me to go to the Parkinsons' next door and feed their cat.

"What's it worth?" I say, pointing to the jar.

Mom gives me one of her exasperated looks. She has no sense of humor whatsoever.

"Go there right now, young man," she says, lobbing the key at my face.

My mother can be really scary at times. It's very difficult to stand up to her, even though I'm about three feet taller than she is. My sister is the same and Nana too, come to think of it.

Trust me to be born into a family of psychotic female dwarfs. No wonder Dad went off to work on the rigs.

I feel sad thinking about Dad, so I polish his photo with my sleeve and troop next door.

Wow! It's hard to believe this house is the mirror image of ours. It's so incredibly . . . tasteful! Everything is painted beige, and the TV is huge! (Ours is huge too, but depth-wise, which obviously doesn't count.)

Jasper the cat is very pleased to see me. His purring is so loud it's like a low-level earthquake (about 3.2 on the Richter scale). I give him a can of Whiskas and then some vintage Camembert cheese and a few slices of wafer-thin salmon that I find in the fridge. It's not like any of it's gonna be any good when the Parkinsons get back from vacation.

Jasper follows me all the way home. He seems really attached to me. I have quite a way with animals, I think.

10:00 P.M.: DEN, ON INTERNET

People do not sell lungs. At least not in this country. They probably do in places like Cambodia, but it'd cost the price of a lung to get there.

MONDAY, FEBRUARY 10TH

3:55 P.M.: INNER SANCTUM

Yes! My *Icons of Metal* magazine has arrived. (The subscription was a Christmas present from Nana. I told her it was about science and would help me prepare for my chemistry exam.)

This issue is a Black Metal special. There's a great article on pinch harmonics, an anthology of black metal bands, and a center spread of some girl draped over an amp with not much on (the girl, not the amp). I would like to hang the center spread up on my wall, but my mom's head would probably start spinning around and spit would fly out of her mouth, so I put it under my mattress instead.

At the back of the magazine are ads for up-and-coming gigs. Why I torture myself looking at these is anyone's guess. Firstly, I cannot afford to go; secondly, I don't have anyone to go with; and thirdly, most of them seem to be in places like Slovenia.

You can imagine my mom's reaction if I suggested going to Slovenia for vacation: "If we ever have enough money to go on a trip, Joshua, which I sincerely doubt will happen due to our 'financial difficulties,' I will go to Costa Del Boring. I will certainly not go to a place where there might be fascinating folklore, stunning scenery, and amazing nightlife."

Anyway, because I'm a masochist, I read through the pages and note that Satanic Warmaster is touring in New

York City in July, which would be perfect for celebrating after finals. Why, oh why, do my friends have such horrible taste in music?

I also see that Children of Bodom's doing an album signing before their show in Toronto on July 11th — a week after my seventeenth birthday! Toronto . . . that's only about two hundred and fifty miles away. Number 3 on my list could finally be within reach.

Oh shut up, Josh. You are delusional.

TUESDAY, FEBRUARY 11TH

4:55 P.M.: DEN

I accept two Facebook friend requests — Furkid Furbaby and Hug-a-woozel. They seem like nice ferrets.

WEDNESDAY, FEBRUARY 12TH

1:25 P.M.: LINING UP OUTSIDE LOWER DUNGEONS (A.K.A. ENGLISH ROOM E12)

Lydia and her friend Becky Calbag are discussing all the Valentine's cards they expect to receive.

"Are you sending any, Josh?" Becky says with what I assume is sarcasm.

"No," I say. I wanted to reply with some witty put-down, but words failed me.

"Like anyone would want one from that loser," Lydia says, sneering.

Words never fail her, unfortunately.

THURSDAY, FEBRUARY 13TH

8:10 P.M.: RANGERS

We are making Valentine's cards for that special person in our lives.

"Don't worry if you still don't have a girlfriend or boyfriend," Shaun says. "Just give it to someone you care about."

"Who are you gonna give yours to?" I ask Peter.

"Probably my mom," he says. "How about you?"

"Definitely not my mom," I say. "I suppose I could give it to this girl I met at the Duck."

"Oh really! Tell me more," says Peter, eyes glinting.

He looks so eager that I feel like I have to impress him. "She's a waitress," I say. "But she's only doing it between modeling jobs."

"Modeling? Wow! What kind of modeling does she do?"

"Lingerie and swimwear, I think. Bikinis, thongs — that kinda thing."

I feel terrible telling such a big lie, but there's no going back now.

Peter watches closely while I write "Dear Michelle" in the card and on the envelope. Luckily Ozzy can't read.

FRIDAY, FEBRUARY 14TH

8:15 P.M.: INNER SANCTUM

I received precisely zero valentines. What a surprise!

Then again, there were no offers to arrange my funeral expenses or test-drive the latest model of a walker in the mail today, so I guess I should be grateful for that.

SATURDAY, FEBRUARY 15TH

11:25 A.M.: PASSAGE TO FORBIDDING GATEWAY (A.K.A. FRONT HALLWAY)

Receive an invitation to look at some newly built retirement units.

SUNDAY, FEBRUARY 16TH

1:30 P.M.: NANA'S KITCHEN

If I didn't go over to my grandma's for a decent meal every now and then, I think I would be seriously malnourished. My mom says she's too busy to cook, but I notice she's never too busy to read her trashy magazines.

Nana is my only remaining grandparent; both of Dad's parents died when I was a kid (not a very long-lived family).

Nana pours gravy on my mashed potatoes, and I almost swoon, the smell is so good. This is probably the closest I'll ever get to a drug-induced high.

Nana is a great cook, but I worry about her sometimes because she seems a little confused and forgetful. When she let me in, for example, I swear she called me Jessica. I have no idea who Jessica is, but presumably she's female, so that's kind of odd.

Her memory for things in the past is spookily good, though. She can remember, word for word, pointless conversations she had with her neighbors back in the eighties.

Today I keep her from rattling on about the day Mrs. Broughton's prize-winning orchids developed stem rot by bringing up a subject closer to my heart.

"You know my dad . . ." I say.

"Mmm," says Nana.

"Well, what was he like? I mean, really?"

Nana looks awkward. I sometimes get the feeling she doesn't like talking about her son-in-law much.

"He was very nice," she says after a while. "Very handsome and polite. The strong, silent type."

"Was he like me?" I ask.

"Um, not really, dear."

Nana must notice that I look disappointed, so she adds, "At least not in looks. Your sister resembles him more in looks. You take after your mom."

Great!

"She was very pretty at your age, your mom," adds Nana, smiling.

Yes, Nana, but maybe I don't want to look pretty!

10:35 P.M.: INNER SANCTUM

I just finished a shift at the Duck. I asked Mrs. Barnes about extra shifts, but she said the woman who does the dishwashing on the other days needs the money for her starving family in the Philippines.

I felt like saying, "Yes, well, I need the money for an epically awesome Jackson!" but I doubt she would have been sympathetic.

Michelle had her hair up in a high, tight bun tonight, and while my sister says it looks terrible on most women, it looked stunning on her. Then again, Michelle could wear one of Mom's disgusting brown cardigans and still look stunning.

I wonder if I should have risked giving her that valentine. I mean, nothing ventured, nothing gained and all that.

But no — she probably got a ton of them. Just about

everyone in the diner thinks she's the best thing since Dolly Parton.

MONDAY, FEBRUARY 17TH

7:15 P.M.: INNER SANCTUM

I take a short break from doing push-ups and practicing "One" by Metallica (not at the same time!) to check the list of things to achieve before I'm seventeen in my leather-bound notebook.

I have done none of them. Zero. Zilch. Not a one.

If I don't get a girlfriend soon (number 1 on the list), I might have to resort to drastic measures like surgery (me) or hypnosis (them).

I do have $66.10 in the Guitar Fund, though.

TUESDAY, FEBRUARY 18TH

6:30 P.M.: INNER SANCTUM

Davey calls to invite me over. He needs my design skills in Photoshop so he can make a flattering profile picture for Facebook. In particular, he'd like his nose reduced.

I say, "Davey, unfortunately I don't think my skills, impressive as they are, are quite up to that."

Silence.

"Just kidding, Davey," I say. "My Photoshop skills are second to none!"

At least Davey makes an effort in the looks department. Ollie once had a piece of salami in his hair for three whole days.

THURSDAY, FEBRUARY 20TH

11:35 A.M.: EARTH SCIENCE

I am having an awesome metal-stardom daydream (receiving an award for fastest shredder in the universe) when someone chucks a piece of paper at the back of my head.

It says "J 4 B??" on it. What the hell does that mean? Clearly, the person who threw that wants to get me in trouble.

I already got a warning in earth science this year for splashing Ramen on my volcano assignment.

I scrunch up the paper and throw it in the recycling. Ha, loser! You'll have to do more than that to get me into detention!

FRIDAY, FEBRUARY 21ST

8:30 P.M.: INNER SANCTUM

I can now do forty push-ups without collapsing to

the point of cardiac arrest. My arm muscles remain as pathetically nonexistent as ever though.

FML!

SATURDAY, FEBRUARY 22ND

7:00 P.M.: DUCK

The Dead Duck is dead boring tonight. Michelle has the flu, so Mrs. Barnes is waitressing. And boy is she a flirt. She sucks up to anyone male and younger than eighty years old like a turbocharged vacuum.

"Missing Michelle?" asks Derek.

"Nope," I say, but it's kinda obvious I'm lying.

MONDAY, FEBRUARY 24TH

7:00 A.M.: INNER SANCTUM

My dreaded alarm goes off and I jump out of bed and reach for my pants, but then I remember it's a five-day weekend! Thank God for teacher training workshops.

Woo-hoo! I can sleep in for once.

7:05 A.M.

Ozzy has escaped from his cage and invaded the sacred resting place of my inner sanctum (a.k.a. bed). I try burrowing under the sheets, but he digs me out with his Velociraptor claws. It's no good. I'll have to feed him.

FML x 2!

3:30 P.M.: MR. PITMAN'S

Mr. Pitman is not feeling well today. When I pass him his tea, I notice his fingers look very gnarly. He must see me looking because he says, "You know, I once had really nimble fingers. They used to call me Nimble-Fingered Ned!"

"Really?" I say. "That's an unusual name."

"Make the most of your youth, son," Mr. Pitman goes on. "It's over all too quickly."

Fortunately, Mr. Pitman does not say: *These are the best days of your life, etc., etc.,* so I don't have to go find some high-voltage jumper cables.

Instead, I assure Mr. Pitman that I will try to make the most of my youth, although it seems damned difficult what with having to go to school, do homework, do other people's homework, make snacks, feed Ozzy, walk people's dogs, slave away doing dishes at the diner, check Facebook, and generally cope with the pile of crap that is my life. I don't tell him all that though. He looks depressed enough already.

"Okay," I say to Minty once we're outside. "We do guitar for me, then park for you. Fair?"

Minty squats to take a pee, which I take as a yes.

Minty and I go to visit my guitar. She is looking as lovely as ever (the guitar, not Minty — Minty looks okay). Anyway, I want to get a closer look, so I tie Minty to Steve's Emporium's drainpipe and go inside.

"Nice-looking guitar, that is," says Steve. I know it's him because he has a badge that has "Steve" on it. "Wanna try her out?"

I can hardly believe my luck. Of course I want to. Then again, what am I going to play? "Spanish Romance" is out — that's for sure. I see a few other guys in the shop looking at me. The pressure is on!

"Just play around," suggests Steve. "Knock yourself out."

Luckily, my hands seem to have figured out what to do, which is good since my brain is being useless as usual. I hammer out a few AC/DC riffs, a decent metal gallop, and some bars of "Paranoid" by Black Sabbath. My pentatonic is blisteringly fast, and before long, the other guys in the shop have come over and are nodding their heads. Is this what it feels like to play a solo live in front of twenty thousand screaming fans?

Well, no. But it feels nice.

Suddenly, all eyes turn from me to outside the shop. Jeez, there's a hell of a ruckus out there — sounds like some kind of dogfight . . .

Some kind of dogfight!

I hand the guitar over to one of the nodding dudes and rush outside, where I am surprised to find Minty attacking Ollie's Labrador, Bongo.

"Stop it, Minty!" I yell. Miraculously, she obeys and lets Bongo hide behind Ollie's legs.

"God," says Ollie. "You didn't tell me you got a dog."

"She's not mine," I say. "I walk her for Mr. Pitman."

"She's f***ing insane!"

"I know," I say.

"Mr. Pitman?" muses Ollie. "Isn't he that guy whose wife ran off with the Safeway delivery man?"

"I dunno," I say. "He did get divorced last year."

"Yeah, my granny lives down the street from him, and she said Mrs. Pitman used to disappear into the Safeway van for hours. Granny was disgusted. She said it was no wonder the bread was always squashed."

"Poor Mr. Pitman," I say. "I never knew that."

"He should've set the dog on them," says Ollie, nodding toward Minty. "Imagine those choppers latched around your balls."

Um, I'd rather not. Thanks, Ollie.

TUESDAY, FEBRUARY 25TH

10:20 A.M.: INNER SANCTUM

Spurred on by yesterday's success at Steve's, I spend the morning designing stage sets for my band in my leather-bound notebook. I have lots of cool ideas:

1. TVs all over the stage, on the amps and the drum riser. The TVs could have static like in that Japanese horror film.

2. Cut-outs of broken-down buildings, bricks, broken glass, and barbed wire.

3. Wax statues — really creepy ones!

4. Stuffed animals, parts of old trees, and vines wrapping around the lights — a possible fire hazard, but I want to take full advantage of people's concern for the environment.

I would like to go on, but I have tons of homework that I should to be doing as usual.

I open up my French book and find that I have to write about my town, its services and facilities, and what would make it better. How do you say "a nuclear bomb" in French?

11:15 P.M.

Just remembered that Mom's birthday is tomorrow.

I will have to raid the Jackson Guitar Fund to get her something.

Goddammit. How am I ever going to be able to afford the wondrous Jackson if I have to keep buying people presents?

11:20 P.M.

On the other hand, I could make her something out of things I find discarded in the house. That'll cost nothing and be much more thoughtful.

WEDNESDAY, FEBRUARY 26TH — MOM'S BIRTHDAY

6:50 A.M.: INNER SANCTUM

Back to the hellhole that is high school . . .

7:00 P.M.: MOVIE THEATER, WATCHING UP

Oh my God, this movie is so sad. I'm having to work hard to keep from bawling. In fact, I am bawling.

Beside me, Maddie is also dabbing her eyes and wiping away snot. Mom, however, remains dry eyed and stony faced. I am now more convinced than ever that she is a robot.

She liked the cardboard magazine holder I made her, though.

FRIDAY, FEBRUARY 28TH

8:00 P.M.: DAVEY'S HOUSE FOR SLEEPOVER

Another birthday today — this time Davey's. His mom and dad bought him a laptop, an iPad, a pair of Nikes, and a Ferrari. Not a real Ferrari, but a cake in the shape of one. All of this kind of puts a damper on the can of Gillette shaving cream I got him. Still, you can't shave with an iPad.

Or can you?

8:10 P.M.: DAVEY'S INNER SANCTUM

I am so stuffed with pizza, soda, and Ferrari, I can hardly move. I gotta say, Davey sure knows how to pack it away. Currently he is devouring yet another family-size bag of Spicy Nacho Doritos.

"Jesus, Davey," I say. "If eating ever becomes an Olympic sport, you'll be a triple gold medalist!"

"Thanks," says Davey, putting the bag down.

Davey is one of those kids blessed with normal parents, i.e., parents who let him have a TV, Xbox, PlayStation, DVD player, and computer in his room. We are playing *Call of Duty*, and I am letting the team down badly. This is what happens when you don't have the latest stuff at home to practice on. I should sue my mom for emotional, physical, and technological neglect.

SATURDAY, FEBRUARY 29TH

2:15 A.M.: STILL IN DAVEY'S INNER SANCTUM, WITH LIGHTS OUT

As usual, I'm the only one still awake. It's hard to get comfy, because Davey keeps flapping his arms in my face and Ollie keeps farting. The last one smelled so bad I'm amazed it didn't corrode a hole in his sleeping bag. Meanwhile, Peter's phone keeps blinking and buzzing.

Will I get any sleep tonight?

5:30 A.M.

No.

LATER

Sleeping — Guitar — Duck — Sleeping.

SUNDAY, MARCH 1ST

Sleeping — Guitar — Ozzy — Sleeping.
One of my better weekends.

MONDAY, MARCH 2ND

6:00 P.M.: INNER SANCTUM

I should be doing some weight lifting, but I can't be bothered. I just don't think I have the type of body that puts on muscle. I should really stop being so pathetically shallow and learn to be happy with my physique as it is.

6:05 P.M.

I wonder if you can get bicep implants . . .

TUESDAY, MARCH 3RD

4:15 P.M.: THRONE ROOM (A.K.A. BATHROOM), SCRUBBING OZZY'S CAGE

Ozzy's cage is now sparkling, but there is one problem. It seems that if you flush large quantities of sawdust down a toilet, the toilet stops working.

Ozzy and I watch as the water swirls around, rising frighteningly high up the sides like a big pot of boiling . . . sawdust.

"Shit," I say.

Ozzy looks up with his beady eyes and says, "Dook?"

"You'll be all right," I say. "Mom likes you."

4:35 P.M.

I managed to get the toilet working again, but it required drastic action, and I am now slightly traumatized.

WEDNESDAY, MARCH 4TH —
4 MONTHS TILL MY 17TH BIRTHDAY

5:20 P.M.: PASSAGE TO FORBIDDING GATEWAY

I receive a free sample of deluxe, ultra-absorbent incontinence pads in the mail. This has gone too far now. I'll have to complain to the mailman.

It's four months till my birthday, so I still have four months to get a girlfriend, see Children of Bodom live, learn "One" by Metallica, get a piercing and/or tattoo, metamorphose into someone cool and strong like my dad, and save up for the wondrous Jackson. Four months suddenly doesn't seem like a very long time.

THURSDAY, MARCH 5TH

7:30 P.M.: RANGERS

"Tonight we're doing music trivia!" cries Shaun. (He is very easily excited.) "I'm sure you'd all like to thank Jess and Lucy for organizing it."

Jess and Lucy wear pink headbands and giggle a lot, which isn't a good sign IMHO. Note to self: they are definitely not potential girlfriend material.

I team up with Peter, hoping he will field the questions on pop, and with Nick Armstrong because he has no one else to go with (largely because he never stops picking his nose). Anyway, not surprisingly, we do horribly because there are no questions on Céline Dion, Broadway, or metal. What sort of music trivia is this? It's crap music trivia, is the answer.

I complain to Shaun, and he says that he's surprised I didn't get the question on U2 since I am such a guitar buff (as he calls it). Shaun goes on to state that The Edge is probably the world's best ever guitar player.

I say, "Ah, but can he play two hundred and eighty beats per minute for longer than five minutes at a time?"

Shaun starts to answer, but I interject. "Can he play while simultaneously singing and leaping off a car?"

"How should I know?" says Shaun irritably.

"Alexi Laiho from Children of Bodom can," I say.

Shaun then pretends to be busy adjusting his neckerchief. He is a really sore loser.

10:10 P.M.: INNER SANCTUM

I'm wondering if I should have been nicer to Shaun about The Edge. I will probably never receive my Musician's badge now.

FRIDAY, MARCH 6TH

8:30 P.M.: KITCHEN

I am exhausted. First I walked Minty, then I had to

walk Mrs. Harris's tiny orange Poodle, Cindy-Lou. I was dreading seeing someone from school, so I stayed on the quieter streets, but who should come around the corner of Duke Avenue but the Lovely (Not) Lydia and her BFF Becky.

"Hi, Josh," said Becky. "Nice dog."

Yeah, yeah, very funny!

I pulled up my jacket collar, kept my head down, and hurried on, pretending I didn't know them. I have a painful bruise from walking into a parking meter, but at least I got $8 from Mrs. Harris.

Mrs. Harris thinks I'm a "lovely young man." Unfortunately, she is over eighty and therefore not potential girlfriend material.

The Guitar Fund now stands at $154.92 plus three Canadian coins and a green button. I have no idea where the button came from, but unless it's worth $650, I am still a million miles from the Jackson.

SATURDAY, MARCH 7TH

6:10 P.M.: THRONE ROOM

It's Saturday, which means, joy of joys, my weekly torture at the Duck Revived. If I had my way, the duck would've been left to breathe its last breath and die with dignity.

Anyway, while other teenagers are out kissing by the train tracks and generally having an amazing time, I will be up to my elbows in soapsuds and, if I'm really lucky, allowed to arrange some lettuce.

I should be getting ready for work, but instead I stay on the toilet, listening to the melodic tones of Cannibal Corpse on my headphones. I let my eyes glaze over, and the clutter of the bathroom blurs out of focus. All of my sister's sprays, lotions, and balms recede from view. *Where does she get the energy to care about things like brittle cuticles?* I wonder.

I'm starting to doze off a little, but suddenly the door creaks open, which panics me into action. Thankfully, it's only Ozzy (escaped from his cage again). Ozzy rolls around happily in the toilet paper which has unraveled onto the floor.

"Ozzy, you are my one true friend," I tell him.

"Dook. Dook," agrees Ozzy.

"Promise me you'll never leave."

"Dook. Dook."

"The Junior Prom is after finals," I go on. "It's not for a long time, but what if I'm the only one without a girlfriend? True, none of my friends have girlfriends, but Ollie and Davey are rich and will be able to bribe someone to go with them, and Peter is almost certainly gay."

6:15 P.M.

Maybe I should say I'm gay. A gay metalhead? Well, the guy from Judas Priest pulled it off. (Being gay that is, not his head.) No, that would be suicide; boys might hit on me. Peter might hit on me!

"Oh God, what should I do, Ozzy? Bestow your ferrety wisdom upon me."

Ozzy jumps up on my lap, but his paws get caught in my headphone wires and he loses his footing, sending a long, bloody scrape down my thigh as he tries to hold on. It will probably leave quite an impressive scar . . . too bad no one will ever see it.

"Josh," calls Mom. "What are you doing up there? It's twenty past six; you'll be late for work."

Well, it's another twenty dollars, I suppose. I wipe the blood off and get changed.

At the bottom of the stairs, I stop to look at the picture of Dad on the wall. Dad is leaning on a gate somewhere — probably somewhere cool like Finland. He is very good looking. Even though I am definitely not gay, I can see that. And his arms are even bigger than Clint's! One thing is certain: I will never be half as strong or cool as my dad was.

6:35 P.M.: DUCK REVIVED

At the restaurant, Mrs. Barnes looks me up and down, walks around me still looking me up and down, and then says, "Hmm. Yes, okay."

Mrs. Barnes believes I am presentable enough to be seen mingling among the prestigious (not!) clientele of the Duck Revived. However, my duties are strictly limited.

"Taking orders is harder than it looks," she says. "I'm not sure we should let you loose on that just yet. But I don't see why you can't go collect people's dirty plates."

"Wow! Thanks," I say. "It'll be brain surgery next!"

Actually, I just nod. I don't have the energy for anything else. Somehow working at the Duck robs me of the will to string a sensible sentence together.

Anyway, it'll give me a chance to lose the gloves I've been wearing. I've noticed a rash developing on my wrist, suggesting I'm allergic to rubber. This probably cuts a whole realm of potentially interesting experimentation out of my future sex life. Assuming I have a future sex life! Deep-sea diving is probably a no-go too.

The Duck Revived used to be a laid-back blue-collar diner, but Mrs. Barnes has decided to change all that and "revamp it." She shows me the new menu, which has been cobbled together in Microsoft Word and has clip art pictures of smiling utensils.

"My nephew did this," she says. "He's only about your age, but he's incredibly good with computers."

"I can tell," I say.

Instead of fries, we now sell Pommes Frites with garlic mayo. Instead of biscuits and gravy, we have toasted paninis with buffalo mozzarella and roasted vegetables.

Derek, for one, is not happy. "I can't even pronounce the things on this menu," he moans. I sympathize, but at least my job of making the salad garnishes has gotten somewhat more interesting. I have to grate carrots now and twist the cucumber slices into little s shapes. If we're not too busy, I think I might even cut little v shapes into the tomato slices. Then again, I might come to my senses.

"Table three," instructs Mrs. Barnes. "Quickly, Joshua. We don't want the flies landing."

I click my heels together and salute her retreating back, which amuses Derek for some reason. I leave him coughing and spluttering into the deep-fat fryer and head out into the restaurant.

God, it's amazing what people leave on their plates. I'm tempted to pick at some leftover cheese, but Mrs. Barnes is watching me like a vulture from the bar. I can feel her eyes stripping the skin from my bones.

Michelle whisks by with a tray, calling out, "Table twelve, three tuna paninis, one baked potato with beans."

Somehow she manages to make the job look sexy. And it seems I'm not the only one who thinks so. I hear the recipients, a group of about four dudes, calling her "baby" and stuff.

Jeez! One of them sounded just like that moron my sister calls a boyfriend — otherwise known as Clint.

I look around cautiously. It *is* Clint!

I scurry back with my dirty plates. If that lowlife spots me, I'll never hear the end of it.

Michelle follows me into the kitchen, looking pink and angry.

"Jerk," she says.

I apologize, but she says she doesn't mean me. Apparently, one of the guys at table twelve pinched her bottom and said that he'd pay her to give him a lap dance.

What a disgusting thing to say. Men like that should be ashamed of themselves.

10:30 P.M.

As I walk home, I wonder if Michelle's sexual harasser was Clint. I wouldn't be surprised. The guy's a jerk, and it's not just me who thinks so; Mom doesn't think much of him either.

Anyway, whoever it was, that was really out of line to ask for a lap dance.

Although I can imagine Michelle might be quite good at one. She certainly has the figure . . .

SUNDAY, MARCH 8TH

10:10 A.M.: KITCHEN

I come downstairs to find Mr. Coles from across the street fixing our freezer. There are bags of soggy vegetables and fish sticks all over the floor.

"How's it going, son?" says Mr. Coles, putting down his screwdriver. "Got a girlfriend yet?"

What is it with these people? They are more obsessed with me finding a girlfriend than I am.

"He's concentrating on school," Mom says proudly.

"Ah," says Mr. Coles. "I should've done that, but at his age, I was out on the town, living it up. Best days of my life, they were."

"Oh yes, mine too," says Mom with a weird twinkle in her eye.

I wonder how easy it is to kill two people with a screwdriver and a bag of half-frozen peas. I decide to go back upstairs before the darker side of me attempts to find out.

MONDAY, MARCH 9TH

4:15 P.M.: PASSAGE TO FORBIDDING GATEWAY

Our mailman tells me I have made his day when I complain about the senior citizen mail I've been getting.

He is laughing so much, it looks like he's about to wet himself. Perhaps if he does, he'll be more understanding about my incontinence pads.

6:45 P.M.: KITCHEN

My sister is getting trained to pierce ears at Fringe Benefits, the salon where she works.

"Great!" I say. "You can do mine."

"You are not getting your ears pierced!" announces Mom with such venom it's like I asked if I can open a strip club in the living room.

"Lots of people have pierced ears, Mom," I say. "Even you!"

"I'm a girl," says Mom.

Uh, Mom, sorry to disappoint you, but you stopped being a girl about thirty years ago.

"Promise me you won't pierce his ears, Maddie," Mom goes on.

"I promise," says my pathetic, goody-two-shoes, wimp of a sister.

TUESDAY, MARCH 10TH

11:45 A.M.: SOCCER FIELD BLEACHERS

"So," says Ollie, "anyone get any interesting mail recently?"

"Not me," says Peter.

"Nah," says Davey. "All I ever get is offers for extreme sports holidays and fast cars. You know — young guy kind of mail."

"Yeah, me too," says Ollie. "Still, it's better that than getting mail targeted at really old people or people with embarrassing health conditions!"

"What is that girl wearing?" I say, pointing to some run-of-the-mill ninth-grade kid in a totally normal outfit. I had to change the subject quickly — couldn't let them know I've been receiving incontinence pads in the mail.

WEDNESDAY, MARCH 11TH

3:30 P.M.: PARKING LOT OUTSIDE THE MUSIC HALLWAY

I suggest to Mr. Trumper that music would be more popular at our school if people could study the various genres and sub-genres of metal along with the classics, world music, etc.

Mr. Trumper said metal probably wasn't influential enough as a genre.

I said, on the contrary, that the first metal bands such as Sabbath and Deep Purple were greatly influential and had roots in the blues and psychedelic rock. With their amplified distortion, extended solos, and basic all-around loudness, they went on to inspire multiple genres such as punk, grunge, and even new wave.

Furthermore, they spawned a variety of sub-genres including but not limited to: thrash, typified by bands like Metallica; glam rock, typified by Mötley Crüe; black metal, typified by Mayhem; and death metal, typified by Slayer and Morbid Angel. Death metal in turn has a number of sub-sub-genres, including melodic death metal, typified by Children of Bodom. Plus there's melodic metal core and melodic death core, of course.

Mr. Trumper said that he really had to go now since he'd left the iron in the oven, but he'd certainly suggest it to the school board.

It'll probably be too late for me, but I feel like I have done a good deed for all future metalheads who are considering their options in high school electives.

11:10 P.M.: INNER SANCTUM

Iron in the oven?

THURSDAY, MARCH 12TH

2:50 P.M.: WALKING HOME FROM SCHOOL

"So, you're really gonna do it?" asks Ollie.

"Yes," I say. "Probably tomorrow evening when Mom's over at Nana's."

"But won't she be kind of, uh . . . upset?" Ollie asks.

"Incandescent with rage," I say.

"Dude, you are looking death in the face," says Ollie.

"Look," I say, "I'm almost seventeen. My mom has to accept that she can't control every little aspect of my life anymore."

"Hmm," says Ollie.

10:00 P.M.: INNER SANCTUM

> *Death holds no fear*
> *For a warrior king*
> *His skin pierced all over*
> *With stud, spike, and ring*

From the album: *Looking Death in the Face*, by Josh Walker

FRIDAY, MARCH 13TH — UNLUCKY FOR SOME! ME, PROBABLY.

6:15 P.M.: INNER SANCTUM

"Are you sure you don't want to come along to visit Nana?" Mom asks.

"Sorry," I say. "I would, but I've got tons of homework."

"We can always go a little later," says Mom. "Will you be done in an hour?"

I shake my head. "No, sorry. Really, I've got tons."

"And you have to finish it all tonight?"

"'Fraid so."

"Well, okay then."

Finally, Mom leaves. I listen for the front door closing, then run to the window to watch her walking down the street.

Great. She should be gone for at least two hours, which means I have plenty of time to do the deed!

6:45 P.M.: THRONE ROOM

I eagerly open up my sister's piercing kit and look inside. It seems kinda complicated. There are lots of pieces, and the needle itself looks a little scary — kind of like a giant stapler.

Hmm. Maybe I should play some guitar to chill out before getting started. I've got plenty of time after all.

7:00 P.M.: INNER SANCTUM

I'm just getting my groove on with my "One" Metallica tab when there's a loud scream from the hallway.

"Please, Josh," my sister says. "It's huge."

"What is?" I say, putting my guitar aside. I walk out to the hallway.

My sister points to her bedroom floor.

"Oh," I say.

"Ugh, it's gigantic, Josh," says my sister, going into a shivering spasm.

I look down at the admittedly pretty damn enormous spider, and then, for some reason, my eyes are drawn to a pile of my sister's clothes on her floor . . .

"I will remove it and deposit it outside," I say, "if you agree to do something for me. If you don't agree, I will deposit it in your underwear drawer."

I surprise myself with my wickedness. My voice turned kind of "evil scientist."

Maddie regards me with a mixture of horror and loathing, i.e., fairly normally.

"You wouldn't," she says.

"You know, I think it's a tarantula," I say. "This one is so big she could be pregnant. They love soft, cozy places to nest. Or so I've heard. Places like . . . piles of underwear."

My sister looks like she's about to cry, and I feel a little ashamed, but I can't back down now.

"Apparently, they have six million babies," I say.

"What d'you want me to do?" she moans.

I point to her piercing kit in the hallway closet.

"But I promised Mom I wouldn't touch your ears."

"Who said anything about my ears?" I say.

"Not your penis!"

"No, not my penis! Jesus! My eyebrow. I want you to pierce my eyebrow."

My sister reluctantly agrees, although she will only do it after I get rid of the spider. She follows me downstairs at a safe distance and watches me deposit it over the neighbor's fence. Then she turns, legs it upstairs like Usain Bolt, and locks herself in the bathroom.

"Sorry, Josh," she cries, "but Mom would kill me. You know how she is about stuff like that. Oh, and by the way — your eyebrows are kinda bushy. You probably don't wanna draw attention to them."

FML!

SATURDAY, MARCH 14TH

11:20 A.M.: THRONE ROOM

Bushy? They are definitely not bushy. I think the word my sister was looking for was "manly."

MONDAY, MARCH 16TH

11:50 A.M.: IN THE CAFETERIA WITH DAVEY

"Do you think my eyebrows are bushy?" I ask Davey.

"Well, stop moving them up and down, and I'll tell you," he says.

I halt my wayward brows and try to look normal(ish). "Well?"

"They're fine."

"Not even a little on the fuzzy caterpillar side?" I press on.

"They're fine!"

"Okay. Thanks. What do you have for lunch?" Normally Davey's mom makes him some kind of three-course, five-star banquet for lunch.

"Nothing," says Davey.

"Want some chips?" I say.

"No, I don't," says Davey. "And why do you always have smoky bacon chips? They stink up the whole place."

"I thought you liked smoky bacon," I say.

"Not anymore," says Davey.

"Okay."

Davey sighs. "Is it too much," he says, "to want to be respected and liked for who I am?"

"Uh, well in your case, probably," I say.

"Thanks!" says Davey, getting up from our table. "Thanks a lot!"

"I was joking, Davey," I call to him. "I like you. And, uh, respect you . . ."

But he doesn't come back.

10:05 P.M.: INNER SANCTUM

Guitar Fund is at $231.76. It's no good. I will have to find another way to earn some money.

TUESDAY, MARCH 17TH

12:10 P.M.: SOCCER FIELD

Davey's not at school today. It sounds mean, but I refuse to apologize to him. He's been in a really bad mood recently.

I ask Ollie how he gets money, and he says, "I'm a paid sex slave."

"You wish," I say.

"Actually," he says, "my parents just kinda give it to me. But you could always get a newspaper route."

A paper route! Why didn't I think of that before?

WEDNESDAY, MARCH 18TH

I'm pretty excited about the paper route. I can imagine myself walking out into the early morning sunshine, birds tweeting (singing, not typing short updates on the computer), wind in my hair, headphones on full blast. I decide to stop by the *Hooper's Times* office on the way home from school.

3:20 P.M.: HOOPER'S

I ask Mr. Hooper if he has any openings for a paperboy.

Mr. Hooper looks me up and down and says, "Is this the sort of job you see yourself doing in three years' time?"

"Well, um, not really," I say. "I'll probably be in college then, or . . ."

"Forget it then," he says. "There's a three-year waiting list."

THURSDAY, MARCH 19TH

7:20 P.M.: RANGERS

Shaun is very excited this evening because it's just two days after St. Patrick's Day. He says we are going to celebrate in a traditional Irish way. Unfortunately, this is not by drinking large amounts of Guinness.

7:40 P.M.

Shaun accuses Peter of not being a team player because he refuses to let some younger Rangers cover his head in green paint. Peter says green is not his color and goes off to sulk with his phone.

I am really enjoying being painted though — mainly

because the painter is Stephanie Nagle who, though not Michelle quality, is definitely potential girlfriend material. It's kind of like having a head massage, except paint keeps getting in my eyes, nose, and mouth.

Stephanie gives me a big smile, which makes me wonder if I should risk asking her out. Rejection would be mortifying, but I'm never going to achieve goal number 1 if I don't take some risks. Besides, I have this sneaking feeling she might find me attractive.

"So, Stephanie . . ." I begin.

"Yikes!" she announces, stepping back. "It's the Green Goblin from Spiderman!"

FRIDAY, MARCH 20TH

9:00 P.M.: INNER SANCTUM

I've been working on a stage name and have decided that Josh the Destroyer captures my personality pretty well. But how should I write it?

1. JOSH THE DESTROYER
2. Josh th3 Destroy3r
3. JOSH THE DESTROYER
4. JOSH THE DESTROYER
5. Josh the Destroyer

I think I like number two the best, plus it has the

advantage of being almost impossible to read. Note: the more illegible the logo, the more metal the band!

SATURDAY, MARCH 21ST

8:50 P.M.: DUCK

I'm on cloud nine tonight. Michelle just came over and told me that my salad garnishes look really professional.

At first I thought she was messing with me, but then Derek came and said, "Jeez, son, you're too good to work here. Them's Michelin tire quality, them."

Maybe I should be a chef when I grow up?

No — I must stand firm. It's Guitar God or death.

> *I was born to set the ax on fire*
> *Make it scream with wild desire*
> *Pain and fury caressing the frets*
> *Growling sounds like a kid with Tourette's*

From the album: *Guitar God or Death,*
by Josh the Destroyer

SUNDAY, MARCH 22ND

3:15 P.M.: INNER SANCTUM

Ollie is over so we can do our math homework together. We figure Mr. Cain must've been in one hell of a mood to assign so much. There are four sheets of equations!

"Jesus," says Ollie, eyeing the questions. "These are friggin' hard."

The questions *are* hard. This is going to take hours, but it won't be so bad doing them with a friend.

"You get started on the first one," I say. "I gotta go to the bathroom."

When I get back, I am horrified to see Ollie laid out on my bed looking through my leather-bound notebook! I feel my heart start to thud and the blood surge to my face.

"What's this?" he says. "Why did you write 'Josh the Destroyer' lots of times in weird handwriting?"

"Give that to me," I say, lunging toward him.

"And what are all these names?"

"Ollie, give it back!"

I manage to grab the notebook, but Ollie yanks it back and I'm left with one ripped page. This turns out to be a good thing, though, because Ollie finally stops being a jerk and hands it over.

"They are names," I say.

"Huh?"

"Of bands."

"I haven't heard of them."

"Of my band," I explain. "When I get one. If I get one."

"I see," says Ollie. "And 'Josh the Destroyer'?"

"My stage name. I was experimenting with, uh, signatures."

Ollie starts to grin. "Like autographs, you mean?"

"Yes, look, you won't, uh . . ."

"Tell anyone? No, no."

"Thanks!" I say. "Thanks so much, Ollie. 'Cause that book's private and —"

"At least I won't if you . . ."

3:30 P.M.

I let Ollie watch YouTube videos of skateboarding dogs while I do our math homework.

All of it. On my own.

I cannot believe Ollie thought it was okay to do that. I would never read anyone's private, innermost secrets. Never.

MONDAY, MARCH 23RD

10:35 A.M.: THE COLISEUM (A.K.A. SCHOOL GYM)

I have to play Lydia at Ping-Pong. Lydia likes to think she's a Ping-Pong guru, so I am going to have to beat her.

It could take every ounce of my concentration, but I have to do it.

"Come on," she moans. "Let's get this over with."

"Yes, let's," I say.

"Should only take a few minutes." She sneers.

"Thirty seconds tops," I say. "Hey! I wasn't ready."

"Is it my fault you can't stop talk — hey!"

The next few minutes are a blur. Literally. The ball is smashing around the table so fast it's like a sped-up cartoon version of Ping-Pong. It's like Ping-Pong at warp speed. Mostly, I am matching Lydia point for point, but a silly lapse in concentration means she is now serving for game point.

"Go for it, Lids," urges Becky just as Lydia tosses the Ping-Pong ball in the air and winds up to smash it. Luckily, it's an awful serve, and I punish it for all it's worth. Rafael Nadal would have been proud of that smash.

"F***!" says Lydia. "Becky, you stupid ditz, you jinxed me!"

"Sorry," says Becky.

I serve the next point and win it easily. "Game, set, and match," I announce. I then dance around a little until Mr. Cox notices and tells me to stop.

6:00 P.M.: KITCHEN

I am still grinning to myself about PE when my sister

puts a downer on things by announcing that she will have to give her piercing kit back because she is being laid off at Fringe Benefits.

Any chance of achieving number 5 on my list is now lost. Unless she gets a new job as a tattoo artist, which seems unlikely given that she's about as creative as a Saltine cracker.

I guess I should be more sympathetic, but these are harsh times we are living in. Besides, she has an interview as a Junior Stylist at Curl Up and Dye next week.

10:40 P.M.: INNER SANCTUM

I want to add Curl Up and Die to my list of band names, but I can't find it.

TUESDAY, MARCH 24TH

8:20 P.M.: INNER SANCTUM

Ollie texts: *Hey, Josh the Destroyer, how's it going?*
I do not dignify him with a reply. I am still livid with him for reading my journal.

WEDNESDAY, MARCH 25TH

Yes! My hair now goes past my collar. I make sure to tuck it in my shirt collar every evening before Mom comes home. Still, I can't believe she hasn't noticed. Or maybe she's getting a little spacey in her old age.

Nah.

THURSDAY, MARCH 26TH

8:55 P.M.: RANGERS MONTHLY DINNER

We made vegetable curry tonight. Peter's mom bought the ingredients, and Peter's mom is not obsessed with getting everything cheap, so we had some decent stuff to work with for a change.

I'm getting annoyed with Peter, though, because he keeps going off on his own to use his phone. God knows what he's doing on it. The games he has are crap. Anyway, I had to chop all the onions and carrots myself.

Stephanie Nagle smiled at me sympathetically a few times, but she is no longer potential girlfriend material. Not since the Green Goblin comment.

FRIDAY, MARCH 27TH

1:35 P.M.: TOWER OF TERROR

"Sarah Clegg, 28 out of 30. Excellent effort. Well done, Sarah."

Mr. Cain is going around the classroom, handing back our homework.

"Andrew Parr, 9 out of 30. Disappointing. Remember you need to cancel out fully. Ollie Hargreaves, 30 out of 30. Fantastic, Ollie. That's the best you've done all year!"

Yeah right, I think. *Not that he did much of it.*

"Joshua Walker. Ah yes, here's an interesting one. Along with your math homework, which was 30 out of 30 — I hope you didn't copy off Ollie! — you appear to have submitted a long list of something. I'm not sure what it is. Let's see, now: Vulgar Coffin, Blood Sukerz (note spelling with a "z," it says here), The Axmen Cometh, Josh the Destroyer and the Evil Goats . . . uh, should I go on?"

I feel my face get red and my throat get dry. A few people have started to giggle.

"There's more . . ."

"Uh, no, Mr. Cain. Please don't go on," I manage.

"Well, I'm not sure about the rest of the class, but I'm intrigued. What's it all about, Josh, huh?"

SATURDAY, MARCH 28TH

7:30 P.M.: DUCK

Mrs. Barnes is making me clean out the garbage cans tonight. They smell worse than Ozzy's litter box.

I sometimes wonder what Dad is thinking if he's looking down on me.

Is he proud or disgusted? Is he impressed at my dogged perseverance or appalled at my ability to sink to any level?

I am prostituting my soul for the Jackson. I wish I could prostitute my body, but no one'll take it.

SUNDAY, MARCH 29TH

8:30 P.M.: DEN, WATCHING THE X FACTOR

Unable to keep things bottled up any longer, I confide in Mom about my epic fail in math class on Friday.

She is not even a little bit sympathetic. "The trouble, Josh, is that you don't live in the real world," she says, shaking her head.

11:45 P.M.: INNER SANCTUM

No, Mom — the trouble is that I *do*.

MONDAY, MARCH 30TH

12:30 P.M.: CAFETERIA — BEING STARED AT (AND NOT IN A GOOD WAY)

It has gotten around school that I'm a sad loser who makes up crappy names for bands.

I didn't think my social status could sink any lower,

but I was wrong. I am the human equivalent of a worm. A parasite that lives in a worm's intestine. A . . .

No, I think that's it.

TUESDAY, MARCH 31ST

5:40 P.M.: INNER SANCTUM

Yes! Just when I thought I'd truly f****d things up socially, I've been invited to a party. Okay, so the whole PE class has been invited. Probably the whole grade. Probably the whole school, including teachers, teaching assistants, lunch ladies, and our ninety-five-year-old custodian. But at least it's not the whole school except for me!

The party is Becky Calbag's seventeenth, and her parents are renting one of those big canopy tents. Unfortunately, there is going to be a DJ, but there is also likely to be alcohol, and even Lady Gaga sounds okay if you're smashed.

I gotta say, she didn't give much notice (Becky, not Lady Gaga). The party is on Saturday. Astonishingly, Mrs. Barnes agreed to let me switch my shift to a different day.

I'll have to go shopping tomorrow to get a present. More money from the Guitar Fund! Also, what do you give a teenage girl for her birthday? I have no idea.

6:10 P.M.

My sister pops her head into my room.

"Excuse me, but can you knock?" I say.

"Excuse me, but the door wasn't shut," she says.

"It was very slightly ajar."

My sister does that thing where she closes her eyes, turns her head away, and sighs. "Have you seen my new mascara?" she asks. "I just bought it, and now I can't find it anywhere."

"No," I say. "Close the door on your way out."

WEDNESDAY, APRIL 1ST

6:10 A.M.: INNER SANCTUM

"Wake up, Josh," says my sister, shaking me. "It's ten past eight. You're late for school."

"F***!"

I jump out of bed, fling on my clothes, shove some Ferret Feast in Ozzy's cage, and sprint out the door. I can usually make it to school in ten minutes if I run like hell.

6:25 A.M.: SCHOOL — DESERTED

I absolutely, positively hate my sister.

6:45 P.M.: DUCK

Things are a lot more relaxed at the Duck on a Wednesday. The customers are mostly senior citizens and people with small kids, rather than young adults. There's more soda spilled and tons of fries dropped, though. Those old folks have horrible table manners! But in general, it's about a zillion times nicer.

I must ask Mrs. Barnes if I can change my night to Wednesday.

7:30 P.M.

Mrs. Barnes says no, I cannot change my night to Wednesday. She needs me when it's nightmarishly hectic, noisy, and full of horrible morons — my words not hers.

FRIDAY, APRIL 3RD

4:20 P.M.: LIVING ROOM

My delightful sister is singing her head off, because she has just received a phone call telling her she's been hired as Junior Stylist at Curl Up and Dye.

6:00 P.M.: INNER SANCTUM

My sister's over-the-top happiness is wearing on me, so I have retreated to my Inner Sanctum. If I'm going to sacrifice my hearing, it will be to metal, not my sister's tuneless squawking.

Honestly, my family's about as musical as some vegetable pot stickers. It's a miracle I can play a note.

6:15 P.M.

One day till the party.
Not that I'm excited or anything.

SATURDAY, APRIL 4TH — PAR-TAY!!!

7:40 P.M.: INNER SANCTUM

I seem to remember there might be some kind of party going on tonight.

Peter's mom is going to pick me up at 8:30, which means I have a little time to rock out to some decent music before that pop-music crap infects my brain. I grab the trusty acoustic and fire up some Slayer.

9:00 P.M.: EAST RIDGE HOSPITAL
OUTPATIENT CLINIC

"And you say you did this playing the guitar?" says the doctor, looking down at my horribly swollen ankle. "How, exactly?"

"Um."

"He pretends the area between his bed and the closet is a stage and jumps around in it," says my sister gleefully.

"That's ridiculous," I say.

"At last! We agree on something!" announces my sister.

"Well," says the doctor, "you won't be jumping around on that ankle for a while. It's not broken, but it's a nasty sprain. I suggest you sit down somewhere safe next time you want to do some guitar practice."

"Really," says my mother once the doctor has left. "You're crazier than the ferret."

"Actually, Mom," I say, "it was Ozzy's fault this happened. How was I supposed to know he'd sneaked onto the sta . . . out from under the bed. Um, is he okay?"

"I don't know," says Mom. "I haven't seen him. But with one hundred and forty pounds of adolescent boy landing on him, I doubt it."

"I didn't land on him," I say. "Well, I may have clipped his tail."

My sister shakes her head and goes off to get a latte. She is replaced by the nurse, who has arrived to bandage me up. She's not unattractive (the nurse, that is). She's actually very cute.

"At least it's not broken, huh?" she says.

"Yeah." I nod. "I don't wanna do that again. I broke

my other ankle when I was thirteen . . . falling off my bike."

The nurse smiles. She is very pretty. "I don't know. You teenagers — you're so . . ."

Wild and reckless?

Brave and impulsive?

"Clumsy and stupid," supplies my mom. "He was riding backward down the concrete steps outside Kohl's. It's amazing he didn't suffer brain damage. In fact, sometimes I think he has!"

"What's that in your pocket?" says my sister, arriving back on the scene with two lattes — one for herself and one for Mom. I note that there is no latte for me, the invalid.

I look down, "Oh that! That's . . ."

"It's my mascara!" she says. "You dirty, lying thief!"

"Um, please sit still," says the nurse.

"Why do you have my mascara?" demands my sister.

"Sorry," I say. "It's for Becky. I didn't know what—"

My sister storms off in a huff, and for some reason I start laughing uncontrollably. "Sorry," I tell the nurse.

"See what I mean?" says my mom.

SUNDAY, APRIL 5TH —
THREE MONTHS TILL MY 17TH BIRTHDAY!

Mom says I have to go to school tomorrow. I am so

depressed, I can barely pick up the guitar. It is only one day before the start of Easter break, but I still have to go, because according to my mom, I "might miss something important." Yeah, right.

MONDAY, APRIL 6TH

10:25 A.M.: FIELD OF NIGHTMARES

No PE for me. No PE for me. Everyone else will get cold and wet, but there's no PE for me!

I am in a good mood because I got a ride to school from my mother (amazingly, she didn't insist I crawl the entire way), and now I'm missing PE. There's something truly excellent about sitting fully clothed at the side of the soccer field, watching everyone freeze to death in their gym uniforms. It's almost worth spraining your ankle for.

But then Ollie spoils things by bringing up the party.

"You missed a great party on Saturday," he says. "Everyone wondered where you were."

"Did they?" I say, surprised.

"Well, me and Davey did."

"Great."

"And Becky," adds Peter. "She kept saying, 'When's your skinny friend coming?'"

"Nice," I say. "Can I help it if I'm skinny? I work out! Well, used to."

"Maybe you've got a tapeworm," says Ollie, wiggling his finger in my face.

"No," says Peter. "It's in your genes. Some kids are just born sticks. Your dad was probably really thin."

"Actually," I say. "My dad was built like a Russian weight lifter — stocky and immensely strong."

"How come you're nothing like him then?" Peter asks.

"Maybe his mom had an affair with the mailman," says Ollie.

"Shut up, Ollie," I say. "Just because I'm getting out of PE . . ."

"Anyway, speaking of bodies — what do you think of Davey?" asks Peter, nodding out onto the field where Davey is running around doing his best to avoid the ball.

"He's okay," I say. "Kind of a geek . . ."

"No, I mean . . ." Peter lowers his voice. "Well, look at him . . ."

It's true Davey does seem kinda different. In the wind, his clothes look sort of . . . empty.

Peter shuffles closer. "Do you think he has issues with body image?"

"Issues with body image? Davey?" I ask.

"He hardly ate a thing at the party," says Peter.

"One Dorito," agrees Ollie.

"Well, maybe he wasn't hungry," I say.

Peter shrugs and stands up. "When have you ever seen Davey not hungry?"

TUESDAY, APRIL 7TH — SPRING BREAK!!!!

Yes! Spring vacation. Kind of typical that I make myself immobile just days before the break — I could've probably earned a small fortune gardening for mom's "people" (emphasis on the word "small"). Still, at least you don't need functioning ankles to practice the guitar, which means I have almost two weeks to work solidly on "One" by Metallica.

I should do some studying, but that'll be second on my list of priorities. After all, I won't need to know about the chemical reactions of metal carbonates when I'm a hugely rich and successful rock legend!

On a similar note, hair is now long enough to be pulled back into a tiny ponytail. Extremely tiny. It's more of a tuft, really, but the potential's there.

WEDNESDAY, APRIL 8TH

9:40 A.M.: INNER SANCTUM

F***ing stupid guitar. F***ing dumb song. F***ING F***ING FRUSTRATION! Stupid thick nylon strings, won't f***ing bend! Fingers hurt like hell — probably permanently F***ED up. And where the f*** is fret twenty?

10:05 A.M.

I realize with reluctance that playing "One" by Metallica is impossible on my guitar. Not just unbelievably, mind-crushingly, finger-breakingly difficult. But impossible.

On page seven of "One" by Metallica, I realize there are some notes on the twentieth fret.

My crappy kid's guitar only goes up to eighteen frets. I could've saved myself a lot of physical and emotional pain if I'd realized that from the get-go.

I open my leather-bound notebook and cross out goal number 2: "Master the legendary 'One' by Metallica." I will add it back in if and when I achieve goal number 4, i.e., acquire the fabulous and wondrous Jackson.

THURSDAY, APRIL 9TH

Ankle: f***ed and sore.
Fingers: f***ed and sore.
Mind: f***ed.

APRIL 10TH — GOOD FRIDAY

Today is Good Friday according to my *Icons of Metal*

calendar, but so far I've found very little that is good about it.

My sister has Clint over, and they are monopolizing the living room. Last time I looked, Clint was shoving chocolates into my sister's mouth! Honestly, I wish they would get a room. Preferably one in an active war zone.

I would go out, but my ankle still hurts like hell when I walk on it.

SATURDAY, APRIL 11TH

7:00 P.M.: THE DUCK

Unfortunately, I don't get sick pay, so I have to do my shift at the Duck tonight. Mom says it'll be good for me to get out of the house. But what she means is that it'll be good for her to have her "me time." I have a good mind to hide all her trashy magazines.

Still, it'll be nice to see Michelle and Derek. Well, Michelle anyway.

7:30 P.M.: DUCK, STANDING AT SINK

My ankle feels awful. Derek and Michelle are sympathetic, but Mrs. Barnes just says, "You don't wash dishes with your ankles, so I expect those plates to be sparkling."

Talk about evil. She and my mother must be related.

APRIL 12TH — EASTER SUNDAY

I receive a package of three Cadbury Creme Eggs from my sister, but there's one missing. "Sorry," she says, "I got a little hungry."

My mom buys me a small egg — the chocolate is about one micron thick. The box is pink, and there's a princess on it (I'm not joking).

MONDAY, APRIL 13TH

Mom and Nana had a huge argument. I heard Dad's name mentioned a couple of times. Poor guy — he's been dead for sixteen years, and he's still getting into trouble.

On the bright side, Nana gave me a normal-sized egg.

TUESDAY, APRIL 14TH

4:30 P.M.: LIVING ROOM

Davey, Peter, and Ollie are over. Luckily, Mom is out. She gets weird if I have more than one friend over at once. God knows what she thinks is going to happen; we're hardly going to have an all-male sex romp.

4:32 P.M.

Oh my God, why did I think of that?!

Anyway, Ollie starts the conversation by asking if any of us likes anyone. Apparently there's a girl who works at the cheese counter in the grocery store in town who's the spitting image of Jessica Alba. Somehow I doubt this, but Ollie is insistent.

"I wouldn't want to go out with Jessica Alba," Peter says. "She's too perfect."

"Also," I remind him, "you're almost certainly gay."

"Hmm, maybe that's it," he says.

"Would you go out with Jessica Alba if she was forty?" Ollie asks.

"Depends," I say, "Jennifer Aniston looked good at forty, but not everyone ages so well. Take my mom for instance."

"Your mom's not so bad," says Davey.

"Stop right there, Davey!" I say.

"How come she never remarried?" Davey goes on.

"Maybe because she's super-strict, mean, and standoffish," I say.

"That'd do it," agrees Ollie.

"Anyway," I say, "Michelle at the restaurant is the only girl for me." This isn't entirely true — the way I'm feeling these days, I'd go out with Ollie's Labrador if it walked on hind legs and wore a dress — but it pays to look like you have standards.

"I think I'm destined to be single," says Davey. "Girls don't go for fat guys."

"Fat girls do," I tell him.

"You're not fat, Davey," lies Peter. "You're just . . . height restricted."

"No, I am fat," says Davey. "I lost some weight, but then Mom bought chocolate for Easter and I, um . . ."

"Stuffed your face!" I supply.

Peter shoots me a weird look. "You know, Davey," he says, "if there's something you want to talk about . . ."

"No, it's okay," says Davey. "Let's see what's on TV."

We spend the next hour watching a show about people in Australia dating in the dark (a useful strategy for me in the future, possibly), but then Ollie says he has to leave. Before long, the others are getting up to go too.

At the front door, Peter turns to me and says, "You really are an insensitive prick, Josh, do you know that?"

11:00 P.M.

Uh, no, Peter. I didn't.

WEDNESDAY, APRIL 15TH

4:45 P.M.: INNER SANCTUM

Mom asks how my ankle is, and I make the ridiculous mistake of telling her it's fine.

6:10 P.M.

Mom asks me to put out the recycling, clean Ozzy's cage, organize things in my room, scrape the mud off my shoes, unload the washing machine, and get some 1-percent milk from the grocery store. My life of leisure is a distant memory.

I get a text from Ollie inviting me to go over to his place on Friday. Thank God.

THURSDAY, APRIL 16TH

4:10 A.M.: INNER SANCTUM

I just woke up in a hell of a sweat. I had a terrible nightmare. My dad was desperately trying to tell me something, but before I could make out what he was saying, my mom sucked him right off the sofa with the vacuum cleaner. Jeez, it was really freaky. I might never be able to use a vacuum again.

No great loss.

FRIDAY, APRIL 17TH

4:30 P.M.: OLLIE'S INNER SANCTUM

"Does it ever worry you that you don't have a girlfriend?" I ask Ollie.

"Not really," says Ollie. "I have something better!"
Ollie reaches under his bed and pulls out an H&M catalog.

"Okay," I say. "How exactly is a —"

The catalog falls open to the women's lingerie page.

"Oh," I say. "I see what you mean, but isn't this a little . . . well, a little sad and perverted?"

"Probably," agrees Ollie, "but when I do get a girlfriend, at least I'll know what kind of lingerie to buy her. You gotta keep up with the latest trends. Girls like that."

"True," I say. "That's very true."

"Take these balcony bras," says Ollie. "It says here that they offer support for the fuller breast."

"Let's see," I say, but then Ollie's mom knocks on the door, and we have to hide the catalog under the bedspread.

SATURDAY, APRIL 18TH

2:35 P.M.: KITCHEN

I ask my sister why we don't get the H&M catalog.

"'Cause Mom and I don't want you perving over the women's lingerie section," she says.

9:00 P.M.: DUCK

Derek let me fry some shrimp in his deep-fat fryer

tonight. He said if Mrs. Barnes wasn't looking, I could eat a few. Yes, living the dream at last!

SUNDAY, APRIL 19TH

1:30 P.M.: KITCHEN

I overhear my sister in the living room telling Mom she needs to get as much practice as possible cutting hair for her new job at Curl Up and Dye.

I shovel down my cornflakes, but just as I get up from the table, Mom appears and yanks my hair out of my collar while my sister blocks the exit. I am a poor, cornered fox with nowhere to run.

I say to my sister, "If you give me a Justin Bieber cut, I will never speak to you again."

"Promise?" says my sister.

2:20 P.M.

It's not Justin Bieber, but it is very short.

Mom walks around me, inspecting my haircut.

"Excellent," she tells my sister. "Very neat and presentable."

Neat and presentable!

FML.

7:25 A.M.: MAIN STREET ON THE WAY TO SCHOOL

I have just heard the worst possible news: Davey has a girlfriend! Jesus, and to think I was starting to feel sorry for him.

Admittedly, she hasn't seen him yet, at least not in the flesh, but she's seen the photo of him on Facebook — the one I helped create. His status now brags that he's "in a relationship with Tanya."

It's sickening. Davey has less sex appeal than a cow pie. A cow pie from a very sick cow that is swarming with huge, bloated flies.

I'm really not coping well with this.

The thing is, he's showing off like some puffed-up peacock. You'd think he'd have more tact. We stop at the crosswalk on Main Street and press the button even though it makes us look like complete losers.

"It's natural too — her hair," he says. "Not bleached. I think that's better, don't you? Natural hair?"

"I guess," I say. I'm not really picky, though. Just having hair would be good enough for me.

"And her eyes are the bluest I've ever seen. Bluer than Megan Fox's."

Oh, come on — now he's saying she's hotter than Megan Fox!

A bus is approaching at a good clip, and I'm tempted to push him out in front of it.

"Have you done your earth science homework?" I ask in a desperate attempt to change the subject. "The stuff about drumlins?"

"Drumlins," mumbles Davey. "I bet Tanya's got great drumlins."

Unfortunately, the bus has now passed, and the walk signal is flashing. I'll have to kill him on the way home.

10:30 A.M.: TOWER OF TERROR

I am still reeling from Davey's news. It's official: every sixteen-year-old in the country has a girlfriend except me.

I'm feeling the pressure more than ever, and it's making me impulsive. Gabrielle Evans is handing out some graph paper. Gabby isn't blessed in the looks department; she has very thick glasses and more zits than a Dalmatian with measles. But she does have nice hair and a passable figure, which is the most important thing. I manage to accidentally-on-purpose touch her hand as she lays down my paper.

Wow! Her stare takes me aback. That is one disgusted stare. Gabby hates me — that much is obvious. I'll have to set my sights lower.

11:05 A.M.: HALLWAY

Alice Can't-Remember-Her-Last-Name is about four foot nothing. I open the door to the English classroom, stand to one side to let her through, and give her my biggest smile.

She mouths a very obvious "F*** you!" back at me, which as pick-up lines go, isn't great. But at least we're communicating.

TUESDAY, APRIL 21ST

9:10 A.M.: EARTH SCIENCE

Becky Calbag nudges me in the back and says, "I like your haircut."

Yeah, yeah, kick a man when he's down, why don't you? Honestly, I don't know how much more of this I can take.

6:30 P.M.: INNER SANCTUM

Okay, so the obvious way of getting a girlfriend, i.e., being nice, has failed. I clearly need to come up with something more . . . drastic . . .

7:10 P.M.

DEATH TO ALL BUT METAL

*~~Attractive~~ Not bad-looking ~~16~~ ~~17~~ 18
YO male, 6'-ish, skinny, athletic, blue
eyes, nice nose, good sense of humor,
desperately seeks young woman ~~16-17~~
~~25-30~~ any age to share a good time, see
bands, etc. Must have own money — I'm
broke, sorry :-(
Call now for a good time!*

Can I possibly send this in to our local paper?

7:20 P.M.

What if someone replies?!!

WEDNESDAY, APRIL 22ND

6:00 P.M.: DEN, ON INTERNET

Davey's Facebook wall is covered with posts from
Tanya. I haven't read all of them (yet), but most say things
like "Miss you" and "Love you" and have millions of XOs.
How can they miss and love each other when they've
never even met!?

I take care of Davey's *FarmTown* and *PurrfectPets*.
Someone has to keep an eye on things.

THURSDAY, APRIL 23RD

6:15 P.M.: KITCHEN

"Jesus!" announces my sister. "Listen to this personals ad. Some loser wrote: 'Fairly attractive eighteen-year-old male, nice nose, no money, guitar guru, call for a good time!' Jeez, what a catch. I bet he's gonna be swamped with offers. NOT!"

"Maybe he didn't have enough money to put more words," I say.

"Huh?"

"Well, the paper charges fifty cents per word."

"How do you know?"

"I just . . . um . . ."

"OMG. Tell me that isn't you!" exclaims my sister.

"Of course it's not! I'm not eighteen, am I?"

"No, and your nose isn't that nice either," she says.

"It's not bad!"

"Guitar Guru! It *is* you!"

I leave my sister wiping tears of hilarity from her eyes. Nice to know my nightmare of an existence brings happiness to others.

FRIDAY, APRIL 24TH

4:50 P.M.: PARK

Mr. Pitman is having a good day with his arthritis today, so I push him down to the park (in his wheelchair, that is!) and he buys me a strawberry ice cream cone and Minty a vanilla one. It's kind of cold for ice cream, but I don't want to hurt his feelings by saying no.

Anyway, for some reason I find myself telling Mr. Pitman all about my lack of success in the girlfriend department.

"No one has a crush on me," I say, slurping my strawberry ice cream miserably. "And apparently my nose isn't that nice."

I am being pathetic, but Mr. Pitman kindly doesn't point that out. "Your nose is fine," he says. "And you are still very young, Josh. At your age, I was playing baseball and listening to music. Don't let peer pressure get to you. A girl will come along in her own good time — probably when you least expect it."

"Yeah," I say. I feel better after talking to Mr. Pitman. I bend down to give Minty a friendly pat, but she hasn't finished her ice cream yet, so she growls at me savagely.

SATURDAY, APRIL 25TH

8:45 A.M.: INNER SANCTUM

It's Saturday! Hooray. With any luck, I should be able to get in eight hours of guitar practice today. If Mom'll leave me alone, that is. So far, she's barged into my Inner Sanctum twice. Once to get my laundry (supposedly) and once to ask if I want a cup of coffee, which is an acceptable intrusion, I guess, given my slight addiction to caffeine.

Jeez, what a pathetic addiction.

Anyway, I played my favorite Children of Bodom album to get inspired for a mammoth daylong session, and then Mom appears with the coffee.

"I wish they wouldn't shout like that," she shouts.

"Huh?"

"I said, I wish . . ."

Reluctantly, I turn down Alexi in full throat. "Yeah, Mom?"

"I said I wish they wouldn't shout and growl like that. The music itself is quite nice."

Quite nice?

"Mom," I say, "please go and put your head under a giant boulder."

I don't really say this. I say, "Well, the growling kind of adds to the overall aggressive feel."

"Don't you think there's enough aggression in real life?" she says, placing the coffee mug smack down on my perfectly pristine and uncreased Children of Bodom limited-edition CD sleeve.

Argh! Mom, please go and insert a wooden spoon up your . . .

"Thanks," I say.

"Don't let it get cold."

Finally, she leaves, and I grab my trusty nylon-string and prepare to rock.

"Oh," she says, poking her head back into my room. "Can you pop over to mow Mrs. Wilmslow's lawn? Don't expect much pay; the poor woman's practically penniless."

I put my head in my hands and feel the life force draining out of me. Did Alexi Laiho spend his youth mowing old ladies' lawns? I don't think so.

2:30 P.M.: MRS. WILMSLOW'S VAST ESTATE

Mrs. Wilmslow presses three dollar coins into my palm and gives me a toothless grin. This is what I get for toiling several hours in the unseasonably hot midday sun, heaving her antique, totally useless lawn mower up and down her hundred-foot-long yard.

"Those are special ones," she says. "Brand new. I really should keep them."

Well, there isn't exactly much I can buy with them, I feel like saying, but instead I just smile and nod and back slowly toward the gate.

"You did do the edges, didn't you?" she says.

The edges? OMG! I consider lying, but it's clear that the edges have not been done. Even though Mrs. Wilmslow is about eighty and probably not overly endowed in the eyesight department, she has noticed my hesitation, and soon she's heading to the shed to get the edging tool or whatever the stupid thing is called.

At midnight I finish the edges. Okay, I exaggerate — it's about 3:00 p.m. — but I've still been here more than three hours.

I must look hot (as in red, sweaty, and suffering from heat stroke, rather than amazingly attractive), because Mrs. Wilmslow offers me some sparkling ice water and a cookie.

"Maybe you'd like to come back next week," she says.

"Maybe," I say. But then again, maybe I'd rather set fire to my pubes.

On the way home, I console myself by stopping by Steve's Music Emporium on Main Street. There she is, my beautiful, blue ghost-flamed Jackson. Check out those Seymour Duncan humbucker pickups. I go inside to get a closer look.

"One day," I whisper, "you will be mine, and I will cradle you in my arms and stroke your slender neck."

A middle-aged woman leafing through some flute music gives me a panicky look and hurries away.

"The guitar," I say. "I was talking to the guitar!" But she's gone and is running down the street.

6:20 P.M.: DUCK

"You're sunburned," says Michelle, loading glasses into the sink.

"I've been working outside," I say.

Michelle smiles and leaves with some clean glasses.

I notice Derek has paused mid-fry and is looking over at me.

"You could just ask her out, you know," he says.

"Hmm," I say.

"What's the worst that could happen?" he says.

I say, "That she starts gagging, and I spend the rest of my life as a sad and emotionally crippled wreck."

Actually, I just shrug and go back to my lettuce.

10:45 P.M.

I can't ask her out. I just can't. It would be like asking Kirk Hammett of Metallica for guitar lessons.

SUNDAY, APRIL 26TH

Peter comes over, but only stays for an hour because he has "to go home and make some important calls."

God knows who he's calling. He makes it sound like he's President Obama's personal secretary or something.

I text Davey to find out if he wants to come over, but

he texts back to say that he's meeting Tanya in front of Target. She's coming from Seneca Falls just to see him. He's planning to take her to Starbucks and buy her a small vanilla latte. *Ciao for now!* he texts.

Well all I can say is I hope she appreciates it. Those vanilla lattes don't come cheap.

No reply from the personals ad.

Is that a good thing or a bad thing?

I don't know!

MONDAY, APRIL 27TH

1:10 P.M.: SOCCER FIELD

"So," says Ollie eagerly. "Did you park your bike in her garage?"

"Huh?" says Davey.

"Plant your seeds in her garden?"

"What?"

"Insert your memory stick in her USB hub?"

"No!" says Davey. "She's sixteen, Ollie! It's against the law."

"So is driving a tractor, but you'd sure as hell do it if no one was watching — wouldn't you?" says Ollie.

"Actually, she couldn't come," says Davey. "Her mom wouldn't let her."

"Moms!" I say.

"You could go to her house instead!" announces Peter as if he's just cracked some top-secret code.

"Mom won't let me."

"Moms!" I say.

"My dad's best friend used to drive a tractor," says Ollie.

Thankfully, the bell rings then, and we all troop inside. I can't wait to go to college and make some new friends; the ones I have are mentally subnormal.

TUESDAY, APRIL 28TH

7:15 A.M.: KITCHEN

We can't find Ozzy!

Sure, he's always escaping from his cage, but usually I can find him somewhere contentedly gnawing holes in things. Not today though. I've searched everywhere. And worst of all, I just noticed that my window is open!

I am so worried, I can barely get ready for school. In fact, I shouldn't be going to school; I should be roaming the streets, rattling bags of Ferret Feast, knocking on doors, and breaking into people's garages. But Mom insists that I go to school.

I currently have 100 percent attendance, and if I keep it up, the school will pay for me to go to the Junior Prom, thus saving Mom about fifty measly bucks. Basically, if I were in the advanced stages of pneumonia, she'd stuff a cough drop in my mouth and push me out the door.

9:20 A.M.: MATH

It's impossible to concentrate. I'm supposed to be solving linear equations in the form $ax + b = cx + d$, but I just can't get into it.

11:30 A.M.: ENGLISH

Mrs. Barber tells me I have a chance of getting an A on the writing assignment if I don't overdo the analogies.

I don't know what she's talking about. I'm about as likely to overdo the analogies as some ditz who wouldn't spot an analogy if it jumped out of her bargain bucket of chicken and landed on her velour sweat suit.

Mrs. Barber then informs the class that for maximum effect, our essays should have strong narrative thrust. This sets all of us immature fools off into fits of giggles.

I feel ashamed of myself for laughing so much when poor Ozzy is missing.

During lunch, Ollie mentions that his world history teacher said a sandwich caused the Titanic to sink.

"Do you learn anything not sandwich-related in world history?" I ask him.

Ollie shrugs. "Don't you want to know how it happened?" he says.

"No," I say, "but I do have an excellent sandwich-related joke. A sandwich walks into a bar, and the bartender says: 'Sorry, dude, we don't serve food!'"

"Shut up, Josh," says Peter. "I'd like to know, Ollie."

"Well, the captain was kind of hungry and decided to grab a quick bite . . ."

I cover my ears and try to slip into a metal-stardom daydream. All of Ollie's sandwich stories are remarkably similar.

2:45 P.M.

I text Mom on my way home from school to see if Ozzy has been found. I have already secretly texted her in math, English, and chemistry. She was not amused, but this is what she gets for making me go to school. Anyway, it turns out that Ozzy is still missing, so I must now do what I should have done eight hours ago.

The first door I knock on belongs to old Mr. Marshall — sadly in no way related to the manufacturers of Marshall amps. Mr. Marshall comes to the door in his plaid slippers and baggy brown pants. He stinks of lavender for some reason, but I push this to the back of my mind.

"Um, hi, Mr. Marshall," I say. "I don't suppose you've seen Ozzy on your travels."

"Ozzy?"

"Ozzy, my ferret. He's missing."

"Have you looked down yer pants?" says Mr. Marshall.

"Excuse me?" I say.

"Down yer pants, son! That's where he'll be."

"Um, sorry. What?"

Mr. Marshall leans closer. "I always keep a ferret down my pants. You never know when you're gonna get lucky!"

I'm not sure if Mr. Marshall is senile, perverted, or just has a very warped sense of humor. Maybe the constant reek of lavender has mutated his brain. Anyway, he's about as much use as a condom made of bubble wrap, so I go to the next house.

And the next. And the next.

No one has seen Ozzy.

WEDNESDAY, APRIL 29TH

7:15 P.M.: INNER SANCTUM

My sister comes in and tells me to shut my eyes and hold out my hands.

Something soft and furry is laid on my palms. I squint down and start screaming. It is Ozzy, and he is dead!

"Oh my God, how could you?" I yell. "OH MY GOD!"

"For f***'s sake!" yells my sister. "It's a wig!"

I look down and see that it is, indeed, a wig — a long, black, silky one.

"We were having a clearance sale at Curl Up and Dye," says my sister. "I thought you could practice headbanging in it. Jeez, you have a very girly scream, did you know that?"

"Oh, um, thanks," I say. "Um . . ."

My sister shrugs and leaves.

Practice headbanging? How sad does she think I am?

8:00 P.M.

It has only taken me forty-five minutes to learn how to whirl my wig around in perfect time to "Ride the Lightning" by Metallica. Clearly, I'm a natural.

If only Mom would let me grow out my hair. Girls would be falling over themselves to stroke my lustrous locks.

> *Locks so long, the girls will tumble*
> *Into my arms for a quick fumble*

THURSDAY, APRIL 30TH

5:40 P.M.: INNER SANCTUM

Davey has invited me to his house after school to do

some studying. What will actually happen is I'll spend two hours trying to show him how to do quadratic equations and failing, because Davey is about as talented at math as sheep are at pole vaulting.

I decide to go anyway, since Mom has been nagging me to clean my room (again!) and also to remove the poster of Alice Cooper getting his head sawn off from my wall. I keep telling her that it's not real, but she's convinced I'm developing sadistic tendencies.

Also, Davey has high-speed Internet access with no parental control and Xbox controllers that glow in the dark.

7:15 P.M.: DAVEY'S NOT-SO-HUMBLE ABODE

Davey looks like he's down in the dumps when I arrive.

"What's up?" I say.

"Tanya dumped me," he says. "She said I might be a forty-year-old pedophile. She says she can't take the risk."

"That is crazy," I say. "She must have seen your picture . . . oh, wait . . ."

"Exactly," says Davey.

Well, I have mixed feelings. I admit that part of me is glad. But Davey looks so dejected that I also feel guilty.

"Don't worry," I say. "There are plenty more fish in the sea."

"But I don't want a fish," Davey says. He really did say that, and he wasn't even trying to be funny.

"I mean there'll be other girls," I say. "And anyway, I've been thinking about all this, and I'm wondering if maybe we're too young to be worried about girls. You know, Davey, there are actually lots of guys who don't have girlfriends at our school. And even the ones who do have girlfriends don't really go out with them. They just hang around school and maybe outside Target. What sort of relationship is that? I think we've been tricked into submitting to peer pressure, and we should just stop and say no! 'No, I will not feel inferior. I refuse to feel like a loser just because some bimbo isn't trying to lick my tonsils.' And besides, a girl will come along in her own good time. Probably when we're least expecting it!"

Davey is giving me an odd look. "Can we do some studying now?" he says.

We study for about twenty minutes (there's only so much you can take of quadratic equations), then we go on YouTube for a little while. We spend forty-five minutes watching people getting in dramatic scooter accidents, ferrets playing the piano (where are you, Ozzy?), and some girl giving a tutorial on how to have anime hair. She's pretty attractive, so we watch that a few times and pause it occasionally.

Then it's back to math for a few minutes before firing

up the Xbox. Davey throws me a plastic guitar, and I spend the next hour attempting to press different-colored buttons in the right order while trying not to listen to "Number One Hits of the Eighties."

Davey beats me pretty bad at the guitar game, but I can't say it bothers me too much. It's nothing like playing a real guitar — not even a crappy little nylon-string for eight-year-olds. Besides . . . I kinda let him win because I felt sorry for him.

FRIDAY, MAY 1ST

6:45 A.M.: INNER SANCTUM

I flip over the page of my *Icons of Metal* calendar to see the face of Ozzy Osbourne leering at me.

My Ozzy has now been missing for four days. I am trying to come to terms with the fact that I might never see him again, but it's very hard.

"It's okay for you," I say to human Ozzy. "You probably never had a beloved pet who was the only one who would listen to all your teenage traumas." I give my eyes a good rub on my sleeve — allergies have been really bad these last few days.

I can't be sure, but I feel like human Ozzy's leer is an understanding one. Personally, I don't believe he ever did those mean things to bats, and I know for a fact that

Sharon likes dogs, so I'm thinking Ozzy would probably be sympathetic.

Anyway, regardless of human Ozzy's feelings on the matter, life must go on. Unfortunately.

SATURDAY, MAY 2ND

9:00 A.M.: INNER SANCTUM

It's May now, and soon it'll be time for finals. I made a studying timeline, but I didn't spend hours on it (like Peter) color coding, polka-dotting, and adding "cool" shadow effects. If Peter spent half the time he did making his timetable on studying, he might actually pass something.

Amazingly, Mom suggested I stop doing jobs for her "people" and take a break from working at the Duck Revived until my exams are over. She said if I study hard, I'll get good grades, graduate, go to a prestigious college, get a well-paid job, and then be able to offer her a life of luxury in her old age.

Uh, yeah, Mom. Whatever you say.

Actually, I've decided to keep working (and earning) as long as possible. Like I told her — it's perfectly possible to mow lawns, walk dogs, shower, eat, and study at the same time.

6:20 P.M.: THRONE ROOM

"Will you get out of the bathroom?" yells my sister, banging on the door. "What the hell are you doing in there? No — don't answer that!"

I have been in the bathroom for exactly eighteen minutes. Admittedly, it usually takes me about three to get ready for the Duck, but I have a few face craters that I don't want Michelle seeing.

"Josh, I am meeting Clint in an hour and thirty-five minutes, I don't have any makeup on, and I haven't even straightened my hair, so will you please F***ING HURRY UP!"

I open the door while she is still yelling. "All yours," I say. "And you really shouldn't spit in people's faces. It's not very ladylike."

She yells something even less ladylike, but I am already downstairs and out the door, so I pretend I didn't hear. Ha!

7:25 P.M.: DUCK

I'm on dishwashing duty again at the Duck. Yay! This is what it's about.

Why would I want to be partying or moshing at some wild metal gig when I can be here scraping the grease off of several thousand plates? At least I brought my phone with me so I can have some decent music to drown out the yodeling vocals on the radio.

Mrs. Barnes comes in and tells me I should stop making salad garnishes and go help Michelle since it is crazy busy out there. "Take these tuna paninis to table twelve, will you?" she says, passing me a tray. "Hurry up. They congeal if they're left too long."

I head out into the dining room and am just about to round the corner to table twelve when I hear something familiar and horrible. Clint's voice.

Jeez, why did he bring my sister to this dump? I hope she's not expecting a staff discount. Mrs. Barnes doesn't believe in them — at least not for lowly dishwashers like me.

Shit!

I dart behind a conveniently placed support column.

It *is* Clint, but he's not with my sister. He's with some other girl! A really hot girl, actually . . . and he's got his arm around her.

Luckily, the Duck Revived has lots of nooks and crannies, so I creep around to get a better view through some vases of dead wheat and stuff.

"What are you doing?" says Michelle, who has suddenly appeared beside me.

"Oh, hi," I whisper. "I'm watching that boy and girl over there make out."

"OMG! You pervert!"

"No, no," I whisper. "That's my sister's boyfriend. She was s'posed to be seeing him tonight, but look, he's with that other girl."

"Oh," says Michelle, inching one of the vases over to get a better look. "Oh, that bastard. Ugh, he's practically eating her face off."

"I know," I say. "There's no way I can give them these paninis."

Michelle nods. "I'll do it," she says.

"Thanks," I say. "You're a lifesaver."

I creep back to the kitchen and try to think what to do, but I can't get my head straight. Maybe I should text Ollie. He always knows what to do in situations like these.

What am I talking about? Ollie won't have a clue what to do.

I text him anyway: *Clint sposed 2 b with Maddie but with other girl. Should I tell her?*

Ollie texts back: *Who is Clint?*

Me: *Maddie's bfriend.*

Ollie: *Who is Maddie?*

I sometimes wonder if Ollie is annoying on purpose. Surely no one could be that useless without trying. Plus, now I have soap all over my phone, and Mrs. Barnes has appeared in the doorway.

"I just received a complaint from table twelve," she

says. "Those paninis were stone-cold. I thought I told you to deliver them right away."

"Sorry," I say. "I got distracted."

"So I see," she says with a voice so sharp it could dice cucumber. "Derek? Put these in the microwave please, and this time, Joshua, get them out immediately."

"Okay," I say.

"I'll be watching," she says. "And I want to see you go and apologize."

"Apologize? Never," I blurt out.

"I beg your pardon!"

"It's just . . ."

"You will go and apologize, Joshua, or you will hand in your apron!"

"Hand in my apron?"

Derek passes me the paninis. "Get fired, pal," he explains.

"Oh," I say.

Mrs. Barnes puts her hands on her hips.

"Fine," I say wearily.

"Tell him he's a shitface," whispers Michelle as I leave.

Just as I get to table twelve, I look around and see that it's so busy now that Mrs. Barnes has had to start serving too. I put the paninis down on the edge of the table and turn away quickly. No way am I apologizing to that idiot!

Clint and the good-looking girl are so totally engrossed with one another, they barely even register my existence. So it's a mystery why I then go and do something really, really stupid . . .

"Why aren't you with my sister?" I say, turning back to them.

"Jesus," says Clint. "What the f*** are you doing here?"

"I work here," I say.

"F*** me."

"Why aren't you with my sister?" I say again. "She's ready to go out — put on makeup, straightened her hair and all."

"What's he talking about, Clint?" says the good-looking girl.

"Nothing," says Clint. "I chucked his cheatin' bitch of a sister last week."

"What?" I say. "My sister wouldn't cheat!"

Clint folds his arms and sits back in his chair. "The women in your family ain't as innocent as you think, buddy," he says.

"Huh?" I say. "What do you mean?"

"Is everything okay here?" asks Mrs. Barnes, materializing behind me like a magician's assistant.

"Fine," says Clint. "Everything's fine."

Mrs. Barnes glares at me and then walks away. As

soon as she's gone, Clint gets up, twists my arm behind my back, and pushes me behind the wheat sheaves.

"Listen, dork breath," he whispers. "If you breathe a word of this to your sister I'll f***ing smash that stupid little guitar of yours and ram it so far up yer ass you'll be burping arpeggios. Got it?"

"Got it," I say.

10:45 P.M.: LIVING ROOM

When I get home, my sister is looking sadder than a Labrador puppy that lost its toilet paper roll.

"Hair looks nice," I say. "Very, um . . . straight."

Mom gives me a WTF look and orders me to take out the recycling. I am tempted to say, "Excuse me, but I've been on my feet for the last four hours, up to my arms in leftover paninis!" but I can be sensitive to atmospheres, so I do as I'm told.

11:30 P.M.: LYING IN BED

Should I tell my sister or not?
Would it hurt her feelings too much?
Would she even believe me?
And how does Clint know what arpeggios are?

SUNDAY, MAY 3RD

9:50 A.M.: KITCHEN

I've decided to keep quiet on the Clint front largely because if Clint destroys my guitar, I will have to practice on a Tupperware container with rubber bands wrapped around it. And I know from experience that rubber bands are impossible to tune.

Anyway, I'm expecting Maddie to be in a bad mood, partly because of last night and partly because, well, why break the habit of a lifetime?

However, it seems she has broken it, because she is surprisingly chirpy.

"Want some coffee?" she chirps. "I'm making a pot."

"You're offering me a cup of coffee?" I say.

"Yes, dear brother. And don't act so suspicious. It makes your eyes go shifty."

"Thanks," I say. "For the coffee, that is. So you, um, seem a lot happier."

She points toward some flowers on the windowsill. "Clint delivered them first thing this morning. Lovely, aren't they?"

"Very nice," I manage.

"His mom got sick last night, and he had to take her to the hospital. He was so worried, he forgot to text. It seems like she's okay though."

"Oh," I say as she puts down the pot.

"Poor Clint. He was so apologetic. There were actual tears in his eyes. He's such a big softie . . ."

I start to feel kind of nauseated, but thankfully someone knocks at the front door, so I am able to escape before she gushes on.

"Hey!" I say, opening the front door. "Ollie, my man! To what do I owe —"

"I get it," he says.

"What?"

"Your text."

"Oh," I say. "Oh, don't worry about that. That's all behind us now. Want something to drink?"

Ollie follows me into the kitchen.

"Yes," he goes on relentlessly. "You meant Maddie your sister. You meant Clint was with another girl and not with your sister!"

"What?" says Maddie.

"Oh hi," says Ollie. "Didn't, uh, see you there."

"Um," I say backing toward the hallway. "I've got this difficult assignment in earth science on plate tectonics. Can you just come up —"

"Stay here, Ollie!" roars my sister. "What was that you said about Clint?"

Ollie swallows. He looks at me the same way Ozzy used to when I took him to the vet. (Poor Ozzy.)

I shake my head subtly, but I am crappy at being subtle.

Maddie gives me a murderous glare. "Stop that, Josh," she snaps. "Unless you want to see what scalding hot coffee does to your balls. Go on, Ollie."

"Well, um . . ."

I couldn't inflict such cruelty on my worst enemy, let alone a reasonably good friend, so I decide to tell her everything. "Clint was at the Duck last night," I say. "He was with this girl. They seemed pretty . . . close."

"You're lying," she snaps.

"Scout's honor," I say, making the little Scout symbol and putting on a goofy smile.

Ollie grins, but Maddie doesn't see the humor in it.

"You and Mom have always hated Clint, and now you're trying to split us up!" she cries.

God, and I thought I was delusional.

But then she takes a deep, shuddery breath and stares down at the table. "What did she look like? This girl? Was she . . . pretty?"

"I don't know," I lie. "She was kind of pretty, I guess. If you like that sort of thing. She had dark hair and blue eyes."

My sister keeps staring at the sugar bowl.

"Sorry, sis," I say, "but you're way too good for Clint. He's a serious jerk-off. Plus you're not unattractive."

(It's true that she inherited all the good-looking genes.) "You'll find another boyfriend soon —" but she gets up and leaves the room.

12:15 P.M.: PASSAGE TO FORBIDDING GATEWAY

Finally Ollie has left. Thank God. Some people don't know how to keep their mouths shut.

Behind me I can hear harsh words being spoken on the phone. "Screw you, you limp-dicked ****hole!" screams my sister. My sister is never one to hold back on the insults.

"Bastard's dumped," she tells me, coming out of her room.

I nod my approval. "You know, he said something really weird in the restaurant," I say. "He said, 'The women in your family aren't all that innocent, you know.' What's he mean by that?"

"I have no idea," says my sister. "Maybe Nana used to be a pole dancer or something."

Hmm, thanks for that, sis.

12:30 P.M.: INNER SANCTUM

Davey just came by to give me some "Missing Ferret" posters he made. Davey's dad works at a place where there are free photocopying machines — or at least they're free if you do it after everyone else has gone home. The posters are pretty good if you ignore the fact that Davey's drawing of Ozzy makes him look like an overweight squirrel.

Who's gonna worry about a missing squirrel, for God's sake? Still, the thought was there.

I have a quick lunch of smoky bacon chips and cornflakes before going out to tape up Davey's posters. I have underlined the word "FERRET" several times and promised a reward of all my PlayStation 2 games. Some of them might be antiques, but Ozzy must come first. Besides, I don't have anything else worth giving away.

11:55 P.M.: INNER SANCTUM

I am finding it hard to sleep. It's hot, and my mind is brimming over with irregular French verbs and the occasional illicit thought of Michelle. It's a shame we don't get tested on sex education for final exams. I'd be great at the demos!

Actually, I'd be terrible.

Anyway, I really should get some sleep . . .

Huh? What was that?

I sit bolt upright, convinced that I hear something down the hall. I stay perfectly still, listening, but there's nothing. Guess I must've been . . .

Shit, there it is again! It sounds like someone trying to break in.

Oh God, who is it? What is it?

I sit very still, sweating like onions in a wok. Being the man of the house, I suppose I should go investigate. Then again, Maddie's right hook is way better than mine, and her nails are like daggers.

Just as I'm about to get up, Maddie appears in the doorway in her Hello Kitty nightgown. Her face is even whiter than Kitty's. She creeps in and sits on the edge of the bed. Unfortunately, it's just us in the house tonight; Mom went to stay with Aunt Sarah in Geneseo who has given birth to twins. That's right — Mom feels that a woman in her mid-thirties is more in need of help than her own defenseless children.

God, I wish Dad was here. He'd take care of any burglars.

"What is it?" Maddie whispers.

I shrug helplessly. "Do you have your phone?" I ask.

"Downstairs. Yours?"

"Battery's dead."

"Well, that does a lot of good!" she whispers.

"At least I didn't leave it downstairs!"

"At least I remembered to CHARGE MINE!"

"Shh!" I hiss.

We are at an impasse. But then I realize the noise has stopped. "Okay," I say. "Go downstairs and get your phone. If anything else happens, we'll call the police."

"I'm not going down!" she exclaims. "Josh, you really are the most self-centered . . ."

I could say, *Well at least I'm not a two-timing, slimy, backstabbing f***er.* But it's probably not the best time to bring Clint up. God, what if it is Clint, trying to force his way in? If it is, I'm dead.

"Okay. Fine," I say. "But if I get killed, promise you won't read the leather-bound notebook Mom gave me. It's got some lyrics I was experimenting with and, um, other stuff."

"I promise."

"I want the Children of Bodom song 'Better off Dead' played at my funeral, and I want to be cremated — otherwise I might wake up in the coffin, and you know how claustrophobic I get. I want Davey to have my collection of oddly shaped smoky bacon chips and Ollie to have that CD we made of us farting to Britney's 'Oops!. . . I Did It Again' —"

"You're stalling for time," she says. "Get going."

I sigh and start making my way down the hallway. I am passing by the bathroom when suddenly there's a loud thud. It's coming from Mom's bedroom!

Jesus, this is scary. There's the sound of repeated knocking and then an even louder thud. My sister has crept up behind me and is holding something black and shiny.

I peer closer. "A straightener? You think they'll want their hair done?"

She makes a face and gives me the finger.

I open Mom's door and reach for the light. "Okay," I say. "Game's up. And don't try any funny business, 'cause my sister's armed!"

"Dook, dook," says Ozzy.

MONDAY, MAY 4TH

12:20 A.M.: MOM'S BEDROOM

So our mystery burglar/murderer/poltergeist turns out to be none other than our long-lost Ozzy! It looks like he squeezed into the bottom drawer of Mom's dresser, ate half a woolen blanket, and then couldn't squeeze back out again — at least not without a mammoth effort.

I'm actually really proud of him.

While my sister takes super-sized Ozzy back to my room, I get a dustpan and broom and start cleaning out the drawer. There are ferret droppings and pieces of wool everywhere. I am just finishing up sweeping when I spot what looks like the corner of a book poking out from under an old sweater.

Wow, it's a leather-bound notebook! Just like the one Mom gave me — only much older. I open the cover and see the words:

STRICTLY PRIVATE — DO NOT READ!

I dive into the middle of the book.

There are some photos of Mom at a club with this eighties-looking band playing. Check out those poodle perms! I skip ahead.

> *Dec. 23rd: Yet another lonely Christmas looms. I might as well not be married.*

Hmm, kinda depressing. I skip ahead again.

> *June 4th: One month to go before my life changes forever! I don't think I can keep this secret any longer. It's tearing me apart . . .*

Secret? Hey, this is getting interesting! I turn the page eagerly, but suddenly I feel kind of weird. I can't help remembering how bad it felt when I caught Ollie reading my secret diary.

I feel guilty, excited, and kind of sick at the same time. Should I read or not? To read or not to . . .

Oh, it's no good, I can't do it. I close the book and shove it back in the drawer under the sweater. I bundle up the chewed blanket, run downstairs, and stuff it in the garbage can outside.

That was written ages ago; if Mom did have secrets, well, they surely don't have anything to do with me.

"Manage to clean up okay?" says Maddie, poking her head into my room.

"Yep," I say.

"Cool. Well, good night."

"Night," I say. "Uh, Maddie. You know Mom?"

"Our mom?"

"She hasn't told you any, like, interesting secrets, has she?"

"Huh?" she says.

"Oh, nothing," I say.

My sister shakes her head. "Well, see you in the morning."

"Yeah," I say.

When I finally get into bed, I can hear Ozzy jumping around and chattering away in his cage. I lift him out and put him on the bed so I can cuddle with him, but he immediately darts away and starts leaping around under the blankets.

It's a terrible thing to say, but for a few seconds I almost wish he were still missing.

TUESDAY, MAY 5TH

2:50 P.M.: SCHOOL

Since Ollie has a dentist appointment, it's just Davey

142

and me walking home today. I find Davey leaning against the wall outside the gym, wearing the same expression you see on men waiting for their girlfriends outside the changing rooms at the mall — i.e., verging on suicidal.

"What's up?" I say to Davey.

Davey shrugs, "Not much."

We wander on in silence.

"PE tomorrow," I say. "Do you think Mr. Cox will make us do squat thrusts again? My legs hurt for a week after that."

"At least you could do some," says Davey. "I barely got off the ground."

"Ha!" I say.

More silent wandering.

"Oh well, when are you ever gonna need to do squat thrusts in real life?" I say.

"I s'pose," says Davey.

"Unless you wanna join the army!"

"Not really," says Davey. "Think I might try to be a financial planner."

"That sounds . . . great," I say.

We've arrived at Davey's place now.

"Well, see you tomorrow," I say.

Davey suddenly turns to me and says, "Josh, are you happy?"

"Huh?" I say. "Well, I guess so. Aren't you?"

"Not really."

I want to ask Davey why, but he has turned his back and is halfway up his driveway.

3:30 P.M.

Happy? Happy? What kind of question is that?

7:00 P.M.: KITCHEN

Over dinner (decent fish sticks, for once — no black spots) I say, "Mom, I think Davey's having a mid-teen crisis. He says he's not happy."

"What?" says my mom. "Well, he should be happy. He's got his whole life ahead of him."

"Yeah," chimes in my sister, "a whole life of misery."

"Nonsense!" says my mom. "These are the best —"

"Stop, Mom," I say. "Please don't say that."

"Anyway," she goes on. "Wait till he gets to be my age, then he'll have something to worry about. I mean, what's left for an old has-been like me?"

"Oh, well . . ."

"There are days when I wish I wouldn't wake up."

"Oh, well . . ."

"Days when I wish I could sleep forever."

"Mom!" I say. "Don't be silly. You're not *that* old."

"Well, I feel like I am," she says. "Believe me — there are no advantages to getting old, Josh."

"Ha," I say. "You're wrong there. You don't have to put up with that high-pitched, no-loitering noise we always hear outside of town hall, for a start."

"I would love to hear it," says Mom.

WEDNESDAY, MAY 6TH — LESS THAN 2 MONTHS TILL MY 17TH BIRTHDAY

6:00 P.M.: PARK WITH MR. PITMAN AND MINTY

This whole happiness thing has been weighing on my mind.

I ask Mr. Pitman if he is happy, and amazingly, he says yes! He says he has some good friends (not just Mom and me!) who come over to have some beers with him. He says that he enjoys the simple things in life, like a good pizza and listening to music.

I ask what sort of music he likes, expecting him to go on about some classical crap, but it turns out Mr. Pitman is a big fan of AC/DC!

"I can play some AC/DC on my guitar," I tell him.

"Excellent," says Mr. Pitman. "I used to dabble on the guitar too."

"Really?" I say, and I must sound a little surprised, because Mr. Pitman says, "You can't always judge an album by its cover, Josh."

Mr. Pitman is damn right. When I saw the cover of

Anthrax's *Fistful of Metal* album, I thought the music was gonna be totally lacking in pace and lyrical development whereas, in fact, it was lacking neither of those things.

THURSDAY, MAY 7TH

7:15 P.M.: RANGERS

Hmm, I still can't get what Davey said out of my head. I'm supposed to be showing some younger Rangers how to tie a midshipman's hitch, but I'm finding it hard to muster the enthusiasm.

10:00 P.M.: INNER SANCTUM

Ozzy scrambles onto my bed, rolls around, and starts making dooking noises. He is very easily pleased.

The trouble is, most people aren't like ferrets; they think about stuff too much, put too much pressure on themselves, and then get upset and disappointed when things don't work out. All of which reminds me to look over the goals in my notebook.

11:01 P.M.

FML!

FRIDAY, MAY 8TH

7:40 A.M.

As I'm walking into school, Davey runs up to me. He looks worried.

"Davey," I say. "Please don't ask me if I'm happy or if there's any point to life, 'cause I'm kinda afraid of what my answer might be."

"Huh?" says Davey. "I was gonna ask if you've done the religion assignment for social studies."

"Oh," I say. "Damn!"

2:00 P.M.: SOCIAL STUDIES

I tell Mr. Higginbotham that as a committed atheist (98 percent sure of God's non-existence), I refuse to study religion or do any religion-related homework on conscientious objector grounds.

Mr. Higginbotham says, "Okay, fine."

You'd think he'd try to convince me otherwise. I mean it's not like it matters to me what grades I get.

Wait . . .

6:45 P.M.: KITCHEN

On the way home, Davey told me that his mom has promised him $40 for every A or A-plus he gets. It's a safe bet, since Davey is unlikely to get even one. I, on the other hand, could be looking at two . . . or even three!

I decide to bring the subject up with Mom over dinner. "Mom, I'm not sure there's much point in studying very hard," I say between mouthfuls of spaghetti. "I mean, who really cares if I get good grades?"

Mom stops washing dishes and looks at me. "I do," she says.

"Really? It means a lot to you then? Me doing well?"

"Absolutely."

"Does it mean, say, fifty dollars?" I ask.

"Excuse me?"

"Well, Davey's mom . . ."

I plow on, expecting her to lecture me at any second, but she just nods, listens, and nods some more. Not once does she butt in with the "financial difficulties" stuff.

"So, um, what do you think?" I say.

"Absolutely," she agrees. "You're growing up so fast, Josh. I can't treat you like a kid anymore. There are things you should . . . things I ought . . ."

"What's up, Mom?" I say.

"Nothing," she says as she grabs her bag from the back of the chair and takes out her checkbook. "Here's some money in advance. Since I know you're going to do really well."

Money in advance! WTF?

"A hundred and fifty dollars," she says, ripping off a check. "Put it toward that guitar you're always talking about."

I am so shocked that I forget to close my mouth, and a huge dollop of spaghetti and marinara falls onto my lap.

7:20 P.M.: INNER SANCTUM

I empty the contents of the pickle jar onto my bed and start counting. With the check, the total comes to $614.32! Wow, just over $185 to go. I might actually be able to do it!

SATURDAY, MAY 9TH

10:35 A.M.: KITCHEN

"Oh, by the way," says my sister, passing me a textbook, "this girl stopped by while you were in the shower. Said you left this in class."

"What girl?" I say.

"She didn't say her name, but she had kind of . . ." My sister makes some weird circular motions with her hands.

"What?" I say. "She had kind of what?"

"You know." Circular motions again.

"Stop doing that," I say irritably. "What did she have?"

"HUGE TITS!" yells my sister.

"Oh," I say. "That must've been Becky Calbag. She sits behind me in earth science."

"That was nice of her — bringing your work over," says Mom, coming into the kitchen.

"Yeah," I say. "Amazingly nice, seeing as she hates my guts."

"Josh," tsks Mom. "Sometimes I think you're paranoid."

"I am not!" I say. "Just 'cause everyone hates me does not mean I'm paranoid!"

8:00 P.M.: DUCK KITCHEN

"How's your sister?" says Michelle.

"Oh, her usual horrible, psychotic self," I say.

Michelle rolls her eyes. "I mean, did you tell her about her boyfriend?"

"Oh," I say. "Yeah, I kinda had to. Anyway, she dumped him."

"Good for her," says Michelle. "And by the way, that was very brave of you last week — standing up to him. I was impressed."

"Oh, um . . ." I say. "Really? Well, uh. Um . . ." My face turns redder than a sunburned lobster, but luckily Michelle has headed back out to the diner.

"You're in!" says Derek, winking at me.

"Nah," I say.

"Ask her out," he urges.

"Shh, Derek. I can't," I say.

"Why not?"

"I don't like her."

"F*** off," scoffs Derek.

"I don't!" I say.

"You're too chicken. That's what it is. I should cut you up into little pieces, cover you in batter, and toss you into this here fryer!"

I used to really like Derek, but I'm a little sick of him these days.

10:10 P.M.: INNER SANCTUM

Oh God, Derek is right; I am a chicken. And what's more, if Kirk Hammett of Metallica walked into my room, I *would* ask him for a lesson. Of course I would!

So okay, I'll ask her out. But I have to do it right. I'll have to learn some really good pick-up lines. Something that'll knock her off her feet. Metaphorically speaking.

SUNDAY, MAY 10TH

10:45 A.M.: DEN, ON THE INTERNET

I'm copying potential pick-up lines from the Internet into my leather-bound notebook. So far I have:

Is it hot in here or is it just you?

This would work well in the Duck since it's usually friggin' boiling, especially in the kitchen.

I lost my phone number. Can I have yours?

Lame, but pretty funny.

You're so hot that when I look at you I get a tan.

Just lame.

Plus one Ollie texted earlier: *Is that a ladder in your tights, or a stairway to heaven?*

. . . Which pretty much explains why Ollie will never find love — at least not with a girl!

MONDAY, MAY 11TH

2:10 P.M.: LA BASTILLE

There are only five more French classes to go! Ever! Realizing this has put me in an excellent mood, but Madame Zizi won't let that last long.

"Josh," she says. "*Qu'est-ce que tu bois d'habitude à midi?*"

I think for a while before saying, "*J'habite dans une maison?*" which has everyone in the class in hysterics, or at least the stuck-up ones. Most, like me, didn't understand either the question or my answer.

"I didn't ask where you live, Josh," says Madame Zizi with a condescending smile. "I asked what you drank at lunchtime."

"Oh," I say. "Coke."

"In French, Josh."

"*Le Coke?*"

Madame Zizi grins triumphantly. Yet again, she has made me look "tray stewpeed." I should be left alone for the rest of class now though, so I go back to the list I've been writing: "Things I've got going for me."

It's kinda sad, I know, but it's supposed to be very life affirming, and I need all the affirming I can get right now.

So far I have:

> *Good at guitar*
> *Kind to animals*
> *Decent nose*

Is that it? God, even I wouldn't go out with me.

Ollie kicks my shin and points to a note he's written in the back of his book: *Wanna come over after school and study? Got new zombie game*, Brain Splatter 2. *It's epic.*

6:10 P.M.: OLLIE'S INNER SANCTUM

Brain Splatter 2 is epic!

10:10 P.M.: STILL IN OLLIE'S INNER SANCTUM

Disgustingly epic!

11:00 P.M.: MY INNER SANCTUM

How are kids supposed to study when there are all these distractions in their homes? I blame the parents.

TUESDAY, MAY 12TH

7:30 A.M.: ON THE WAY TO SCHOOL

Davey is seeing a therapist! She told him to start keeping a journal of his feelings, so his mom bought him a large leather-bound notebook.

"Cool," I say, pretending like it's a novel idea. "It'll be like a release valve."

"That's what my therapist said!" exclaims Davey.

Jesus, I hope Davey's therapist isn't my mom in disguise!

WEDNESDAY, MAY 13TH

8:00 P.M.: DEN

I spend the evening simultaneously studying earth science and pick-up lines. I hope I don't get them mixed up!

Question: *What is the difference between the focus and the epicenter of an earthquake?*

Answer: *Wow, your dad must've been a baker, because you've got great buns!*

THURSDAY, MAY 14TH

7:30 P.M.: RANGERS

We're making animals out of fruit this evening. I got the wrong idea and brought a can of peaches, but Peter is kindly sharing his pineapple with me.

"What should we use for eyes?" I say.

"Whatever you want," Peter replies.

"Well, you must have some ideas," I say.

"I have bigger concerns," says Peter.

"Okay," I say. "Let's try these olives . . ."

"I owe a gay chat line $495.50," says Peter suddenly. "And if I don't pay it in ten days, I'm going to court."

"What?"

"My dad will kill me. He doesn't even know I'm almost certainly gay!" Peter says.

"God," I say. "Well, um, don't you have any savings?"

Peter looks down and shakes his head. I slice the olives into rings and stick two on the pineapple.

"I'm going to prison," wails Peter, tears spilling onto

his cheeks. "Juvie. They'll make me do terrible things like bricklaying and mechanics!"

"No. I'll give you the money," I say.

"Really? Oh God, thanks, Josh. Thank you. I'll pay you back."

"Yeah, well, I meant I'll lend you the money," I say.

"It might take a while, what with college tuition . . ."

Great . . .

10:10 P.M.: INNER SANCTUM

I take $495.50 from my precious Guitar Fund and stuff it in my pencil case for Peter. I am not a wuss, so I don't cry, but it's a close call. Peter better not call me an insensitive prick again, that's all I can say.

SATURDAY, MAY 16TH

5:00 P.M.: DEN

My sister says Curl Up and Dye is expanding its services. They will soon be offering eyebrow tinting, facials, and waxing.

"What about piercing?" I say, remembering number 5 on my list of things to achieve.

"Probably," she says, "but I'm not sure I'll be working there much longer."

"Why not?" I say.

My sister shudders. "Because I have to start doing people's backs, sacks, and cracks."

7:00 P.M.: DUCK

Michelle is out today, which is actually somewhat of a relief, because I still haven't decided which pick-up line to use. On the bright side, Mrs. Barnes has raised my hourly wage. I now get $7.98 an hour, so tonight I'll have almost $33.00 to put in the sadly depleted pickle jar.

SUNDAY, MAY 17TH

Message from Peter @PeterTheTweeter11: *Hey guys, I'm on Twitter! Follow me!*

Message from me: *No.*

MONDAY, MAY 18TH

2:00 P.M.: ART HALLWAY

Art final today. My chosen topic was "The Beauty of Sound," and I have just spent the last six hours painting a scantily clad woman draped over an amp.

Lydia Smart comes up to me, nods at the picture, and says, "She's not beautiful. She's a tramp."

Lydia is jealous because her picture isn't as good as mine. Also she's flat-chested.

I say, "Yeah, well, that's what you say."

Which as insults go, wasn't great, but thankfully Lydia waltzes off, leaving me to enjoy a metal-stardom daydream in which lots of very un-flat-chested women show their appreciation of my artwork and guitar skills!

10:15 P.M.: INNER SANCTUM

Yes! I finally figured out what I'll say to Michelle next Saturday: "It's hot in here . . . but that's just you, Michelle. Because when I see you it's like the sun comes out in my head. You are the reason for global warming — but in a good way. Please let me take you away from all this?" Gesture toward dirty plates, Derek, etc.

I'm scared shitless, but I'm determined to go through with it. Whatever happens, at least I can say I gave it a try.

TUESDAY, MAY 19TH

12:30 P.M.: SOCCER FIELD

Davey's therapist told Davey it's tough being a teen. No shit!

WEDNESDAY, MAY 20TH

3:00 P.M.

Went to my last ever geometry class today! This has put me in a stupendous mood. I say farewell to Ollie and jog home. Jasper, the friendly cat from next door, meets me outside the house and follows me into the front hallway.

"Hey, dude, you come for a visit?" I say, reaching down to ruffle his fur. "So how's it hangin'? You been chillin' with da ladeez? Swingin' that furry —"

"Uh," says Mom, "Michelle from the Duck is in the living room."

Jesus, what is Michelle doing here? Apart from thinking I'm a complete and utter moron, that is. Still, maybe she didn't hear.

I go into the living room and find Michelle sitting on our sofa.

"Hi." She grins. "How's it hangin'?"

Great!

"Um, fine," I manage, sitting down in the armchair. "So, how come you're here? Not that it isn't nice to see you, of course!"

"Mrs. Barnes sent me," Michelle explains. "I'm sorry, Josh, but she asked me to tell you not to come back to work."

"What?" I say. "Why?"

Michelle looks awkward. "It's not that you did a bad job," she says. "It's just, well, that dude Clint . . ."

"Go on," I say.

"Well, he complained about you hassling his girlfriend."

"What?" I say. "That's bull."

"I know," says Michelle. "The guy's a complete nut-job."

"Damn," I say.

"I told Mrs. Barnes you'd never do something like that. I told her you were way too nice. But he comes in most days at lunch, you see. He's a good customer."

"Great," I say.

"Well," Michelle says, getting up. "I'm sorry, Josh. For what it's worth, I'll really miss you. Take it easy, okay?"

"Oh, right," I say. "Um . . . um, it's hot in here . . ."

"Sorry?" she says.

I take a deep breath and clear my throat. "What I mean to say, Michelle, is that I really like —"

"Cup of coffee, dear?" says my mom, appearing in the living room doorway with a pile of clothing in her arms. "I just need to put these dirty underwear in the wash for Josh, then I'll get the coffee maker going."

"Oh, um, no thanks," says Michelle. "I better get going. I start my shift in twenty minutes."

"Uh . . ." I say. "Um."

"No problem, hon," interrupts my mom. "I'll get the door for you."

My mom leads Michelle through the hall and opens the front door. "All right, dear. Thanks for stopping by!" she calls.

KITCHEN — 3 MINUTES LATER

My mother is shaking her head and has her hands on her hips. "How did you manage to get fired from a job washing dishes?" she exclaims.

"Mom, it was because of Clint. He's getting back at me for Maddie breaking up with him," I explain.

"Well, as much as I am no fan of Clint, I don't see what he has to do with you being fired. You can either wash dishes or you can't."

"Mom, of course I can friggin' wash dishes!"

"Don't swear at me, Josh."

"I said friggin'. Friggin' is not a swear word!"

"Stop that!"

"I'm going to do some studying," I say. "Oh, and awesome job on the underwear thing, by the way. I hope you realize you've completely ruined the one chance I've ever had of getting a decent girlfriend. Or any girlfriend, come to think of it!"

I storm upstairs, shut the door, and punch my pillow over and over until I'm exhausted.

THURSDAY, MAY 21ST — LAST DAY OF PRISON!

3:15 P.M.: DAVEY'S BACKYARD

I'm still depressed about losing my job and Michelle, but it's damn well not gonna stop me celebrating the fact that school is over for the year.

Yep, compulsory education is history! Never again will I have to wear this incredibly unflattering snot-colored backpack Mom gave me. Never again will I have to listen to Mr. Cain drone on about obtuse angles or watch Madame Zizi get animated over reflexive verbs.

All this would be fantastic if it really happened that way. Unfortunately, while the state says I can decide to quit school once I'm seventeen, my mom does not say so. In fact, she would kill me.

"Do you think it's safe?" Davey says. "I mean, we don't want to set the garage on fire."

"It's fine," I say. "Throw 'em on."

Davey tosses his PE shorts on the pile of dry branches. "Goodbye and good riddance!" he announces.

"See you in hell!" says Ollie, tossing his PE T-shirt on the pile.

"Your turn, Peter," Davey says.

Peter looks awkward. "Um, I think I might keep mine," he says. "I think the shorts look good on me, and I can coordinate the T-shirt with several other outfits."

"Peter," I say seriously. "This is the ceremonial burning of the PE outfits. We agreed we'd do this. No more mandatory PE next year."

"You can have my socks?" he offers.

"Fine," I say. "I guess that'll have to do."

Davey lights the pile of clothing, and we watch as it kind of . . . chars. It's not really the effect we were going for, but it's still, um . . .

"Very symbolic," coughs Ollie, waving away the fumes.

"Yes," I say.

"What does it actually symbolize though?" Peter asks.

"It symbolizes freedom from the tyranny of PE teachers and other despots the world over," says Ollie, which I thought was pretty good, considering he'll probably get a C in English at best.

Then Davey's mom comes out of the garden and empties a bucket of water over the smoldering pile.

"You four are complete nincompoops," she tuts before going back inside.

"Despot," mutters Davey.

After the semi-success of the PE uniform sacrifice, we decide to head down to the railroad tracks for celebratory drinks, lounging around, and flirting with girls . . . well, lounging around anyway.

As usual, Mom has forbidden me from drinking

alcohol. She says it only leads to trouble and that I could get arrested for being underage. But Mom is still on my bad side from yesterday, so I have no intention of doing what she says. Besides, if I start drinking now, I'll have plenty of time to sober up before going home.

4:30 P.M.: BY THE RAILROAD TRACKS

"Wow," I say, observing the crowd of kids.

"Let's mingle!" cries Ollie, racing off.

"How charming," says Davey. "Obviously he doesn't want to be seen with losers like us."

"Well, maybe we should mingle," I say. "After all, we're hardly gonna get girls coming up to us voluntarily. Let's split up, try our luck, and meet up here in an hour."

"Okay." Davey shrugs. He and Peter head off in the direction of the woods, presumably to flirt with some squirrels.

I feel kind of lonely and am just starting to wonder if the mingling thing was such a good idea when someone taps my shoulder and says, "Hey, you're Josh, aren't you?"

I turn around and recognize a girl from school. She's not Michelle, but she is pretty cute in a chubby, beady-eyed kinda way — kind of like a giant guinea pig.

"That picture you drew for the art final was awesome," she says.

"Thanks," I say.

"So, do you wanna sit down and have some beer?"

"Do ferrets have whiskers?" I say.

"What?" she says.

"Yes, please," I say.

I sit down next to the girl (whose name escapes me) and try to think of a good conversation topic. She's definitely potential girlfriend material despite the guinea pig similarities.

She smiles at me, and I notice her bra strap slip off her shoulder.

"Nice bra," I say. "I'm guessing you get your underwear from H&M."

"You're kinda weird, aren't you?" she says, giggling. "Have some more beer."

"Thanks," I say, chugging some down. "So, is it a balcony bra you're wearing?"

"Huh?"

"To offer more, um, support."

The girl shuffles closer. "Would you like to see?"

"Uh," I say. "That would be nice."

I finish off the beer. I'm just about to squint down her shirt when she jumps back like a startled pigeon.

"What's going on?" says a tall Clint-like person.

"Oh, hi," I say. "Who are you?"

"I'm Amber's brother."

"Who's Amber? Oh . . . right."

"Who the f*** is this?" the boy asks Amber.

Amber shrugs. "His name's Josh."

"That's me," I say, hiccupping. "Josh the Destroyer!"

Amber's brother gives me a WTF look, then takes his sister's arm. "Come on. What would Dad say if he saw you like this?"

"It was his fault," Amber says, pointing at me. "He pricked my drink."

"Spiked, I think you mean," I say. "I spiked your drink."

"You're in big trouble, kid," says the Clint-like one, letting go of Amber and grabbing me.

"Ow," I squeak. "That's kinda tight. Look, the beer wasn't even mine. It was hers. If anything, she was trying to get me drunk . . ."

5:05 P.M.

I'm sure there must be a law against shoving someone headfirst into a garbage can, but it's probably not worth pressing charges. Anyway, luckily everyone around here refuses to dispose of their trash correctly, so the thing was mostly empty.

Mostly.

I peel a used condom off my forehead and watch Amber being dragged away by her brother.

"Hey, Josh. Tough break."

It's Charlene — the girl who was too cool for Rangers. At first, I don't recognize her, since she is wearing purple leggings and a bright pink T-shirt with the words "Soul Diva" on it.

"Hi," I say.

"Yo," she says, sitting down.

"You look . . . different," I say. "You still into metal?"

"Nah, I'm into 50 Cent now."

"50 Cent!"

"And Wu-Tang Clan."

"Wu-Tang Clan!!"

I feel like I've been stabbed in the chest. "But all the concerts you went to," I splutter. "Your Pantera tattoo!"

"Oh, that was just drawn in pen."

Pen! "What about your nose stud?"

"Stuck it on with tape. Do you really think my parents would let me have a nose stud? I was fourteen!"

I am totally speechless.

"Well," she says, removing a gross-looking Popsicle stick from behind my ear and getting up. "Enjoy the rest of the party. And, uh, keep metal, dude."

Ha! Yes, I will keep metal! Unlike some people.

God, people like that make me sick. They should be killed, cryogenically frozen, brought back to life, and then killed again!

5:40 P.M.

"Why are you shredding that stick?" says Peter.

"No reason," I tell him.

"You seem kinda mad."

"I'm not mad. I'm disappointed," I tell him. "People around here are seriously messed up. I mean, seriously!"

"Fair enough," says Peter. "And, uh, speaking of messed up — can you help me find Davey? I think he got wasted and collapsed somewhere."

5:45 P.M.

It's been just over an hour since I saw Davey, so how he could've become piss drunk already is beyond me. Then again, I'm not feeling too great myself.

I look up to see Ollie wandering toward us, swinging a white grocery bag.

"Booze," he announces happily. "My bro bought it for us. Where's Davey?"

"I don't know," says Peter. "I think he's lost."

"Oh, he must be around here somewhere," I say. "I'll call his cell."

I find my phone and manage to call Davey's number. There's some sniffling on the other end and a kind of grunt.

"I think a raccoon stole his phone," I tell them.

"Nah," says Ollie. "Their paws are too big for the buttons. Ha!"

"Davey," I say into the phone. "Where are you?"

There's some more sniffling, then Davey's unsteady voice comes on and says, "I'm in a bush."

"He's in a bush," I tell the others.

We look around at the millions of bushes around the train tracks.

"Which one?" says Ollie.

8:30 P.M.: STILL BY THE TRAIN TRACKS —
ONE GROCERY BAG OF BOOZE AND MANY
BUSHES LATER

"Ask him to describe the bush in more detail," urges Peter between hiccups.

"What is the bush actually like?" I ask Davey on the phone.

Davey says, "It's green. Can you come soon? I feel kinda sick."

"Let's go up here," slurs Ollie, pointing to an area farther down the tracks that is lacking in bushes, but full of girls and booze.

Suddenly Peter stops and squints into the distance. "That's not your mom, is it?" he says.

"Huh?" I say. "Nah . . ."

I stare ahead. About a hundred feet away is a short,

sinister, Victorian sort of woman striding our way. In other words, it is my mom . . . and I'm really drunk!

I look around, but there is nowhere to hide aside from one very large bush about thirty feet away.

"In there," I say. "Quick!"

8:40 P.M.: A BUSH

"Joshua, I know you're in there," says my mom.

"How does she know that?" whispers Peter.

"Because his sneakers are sticking out," replies my mom.

"You idiot," slurs Ollie. "You've given our position away to the ellen, emen . . ."

"Hi, Mom," I say as I get out of the bush and brush off a few twigs and something that smells disturbingly like dog poo. "What brings you to the railroad tracks on such a glori—hic . . . burp?"

"You're drunk," says my mom.

"No," I say. "Nooo! I've only had one can of beer."

"And about half a pint of Jack Daniels and several Bacardi Breezers," adds Peter.

"Shut up, Peter," I say.

"Where's Davey?" asks my mom.

"And a can of Miller Lite and two piña coladas," continues Peter.

"Shut up, Peter!"

"Oh, hi there," says Davey, appearing out from under the same bush. "Sorry — were you looking for me? I fell asleep."

9:15 P.M.: PASSAGE TO FORBIDDING GATEWAY

My mother just marched all my friends and me right down the train tracks, through the adjacent park, and to her car. There were still lots of people from school hanging around, and they saw all of it.

Annoyingly, my friends seemed too drunk to appreciate the horror of what was happening, but I sobered up to feel every mortifying moment.

"I think you'd better go to your room," says my mom once we're home.

"Okay," I say.

"I'm not mad," she says. "I'm disappointed. Haven't I told you a million times the trouble alcohol causes?"

"Yes, Mom," I say. "And I'm sorry, okay? But why is it such a huge deal? I just don't —"

"One day I'll tell you," says Mom, turning away sharply. "Maybe one day soon . . ."

FRIDAY, MAY 22ND

5:00 P.M.: KITCHEN

We are supposed to dress really nicely for the Junior

Prom. Mom starts saying that if I used some of my Duck money I could get a nice, new shirt, but I think she sees from my expression that nothing this side of a mental breakdown will make me spend the Guitar Fund on clothes.

"Mr. Pitman was asking for you," she says, passing over a cheese sandwich, which is presumably my dinner. "He said you two have been having some nice trips down to the park."

"Yeah, he's a cool enough dude," I say.

Mom smiles. "I think Minty may be due for a walk."

"Hmm, well I think Minty will have to wait awhile," I tell her. "Soon it'll be summer, and then I can walk her every day."

Hold it, Josh, what are you saying?

"Or at least a couple of times a week," I add quickly.

There's a large hair in my sandwich, but it looks like one of Ozzy's, so I keep eating.

"It'd be great if you could give the poor thing a quick walk around the block," Mom says in an emotionally blackmailing sort of way. "Just a few minutes. I'm stopping by Mr. Pitman's around six if you want to come along. He'd love to see you."

"Mom," I say sternly. "I'm about to take ten exams. I think I need to concentrate my efforts on those, don't you? Now if you'll excuse me, I'm going to study."

It's annoying, because I was planning on doing some Facebook stalking, but the computer is downstairs and Mom'll be hovering, so I go upstairs and begin studying for earth science. Apparently some kinds of rocks can neutralize the acidity of rain. God, this is boring.

I decide to take a quick break and check the old Guitar Fund. Just to see how it's coming along.

$190.32.

This wouldn't be too bad, except now — thanks to that jerk Clint — I no longer have a real job. Great! I'll need to mow about a hundred more lawns and trim all their edges to get anywhere near the Jackson. I feel so annoyed that I send Peter an angry text demanding that he start paying me back immediately.

I then find the Extra Special Peanut Butter Fudge Mrs. Simpkins gave me for watering her geraniums, and I devour the whole box in about three minutes. I notice absently that two pieces of fudge is 150 percent of my daily saturated fat. I have eaten six pieces, which means I probably should be dead, but so what? In fact, I wish I was dead. Maybe if I had a stroke or a heart attack, people might realize how mean they've been to me. Mom would feel all guilty and . . . and . . . oh God, what am I saying?

I mutter a quick apology to Dad and check the clock. It's five to six.

"Hold on, Mom," I call. "I'm coming."

6:10 P.M.: MR. PITMAN'S

Minty certainly is happy to see me. She tears around the room like a psychotic fly and snaps affectionately at my ankles.

"Minty loves you," says Mr. Pitman. "And dogs are a very good judge of character."

I smile and go get Minty's leash from the kitchen.

"Mr. Pitman used to be a plumber," says Mom when I get back.

"Really," I say. I'm not sure why Mom has alerted me to this particular piece of information. It's almost like she thinks I should be impressed. Impressed by a career unclogging toilets? I think not . . .

"A very good one too," she goes on.

"Ah, well," says Mr. Pitman, waving his hand. "I did okay. Course, when the arthritis got hold of my hands, I had to retire early."

I make a sympathetic noise.

"You know, Josh, I think it's about time you called Mr. Pitman 'Ned,' seeing as you two are getting along so well," says Mom.

"Um, okay," I say. "Ned it is."

Mom smiles. She has done a lot of smiling today, and it's making me nervous.

"Well, uh, I'll just go out with Minty then," I say.

"Yes, all right," says Mom. "You're a good boy, Josh."

I have just started walking when I get a text from Peter, probably moaning because I was rude to him.

Peter says, *Dont worry Hav already got $17.35 4u!*

$17.35. Woo-hoo!

Still, it's a start, I s'pose.

Minty starts yapping and pulling on her leash, so I say, "All right, Minty, let's go."

6:30 P.M.: STEVE'S MUSIC EMPORIUM ON MY WAY TO THE PARK

The Jackson is gone!

I press my nose up against the window, rub my eyes, and look again, but it's still gone. Recently too. They haven't even taken the stand out of the window yet. There it sits, mocking me with its black metal emptiness.

I take a deep breath and steady myself against the wall. Well, it was inevitable. It couldn't wait forever. Some spoiled kid probably got it for his third birthday or something.

I feel my allergies coming on again, but I manage to keep them at bay with my sleeve and lots of sniffing.

Minty gives me a consoling look and pees next to the Emporium's drainpipe.

"Good girl, Minty," I say. "Sure you don't wanna do anything else?"

Minty barks, and I let her drag me to the park where hopefully she will chase and snap at some small children while I annoy the adults by monopolizing a swing and wallowing in my misery.

10:15 P.M. INNER SANCTUM

I open my notebook and put several thick lines through goal number 4.

> *Destined to be apart are we*
> *No more will I see your perfection*
> *Wrenched asunder, I mourn your loss*
> *Like a man who can't get an erection*

> **From the album: *Mournful Loss,* by Josh the Destroyer**

SATURDAY, MAY 23RD

6:35 P.M.: KITCHEN

For most of the day, I continue to mourn the loss of my beautiful, amazing, awesome Jackson. But unfortunately life and studying must go on.

Or so I'm told. FML.

SUNDAY, MAY 24TH

11:00 A.M.: INNER SANCTUM

I'm studying the Pythagorean theorem. Outside, car doors slam as people prepare to go down to the beach for the day. It must be seventy-five degrees out there. The sun streams into my room and dances on my math textbook like a sadistic fairy.

Whoever decided to hold final exams at the beginning of summer should be dragged through the streets naked and then have a stake driven through their still-beating heart.

I study until my mind can take no more of Pythagoras and then start on the past imperfect tense.

I can forgive the French for most things — eating frogs, the Hundred Years' War, berets — but I cannot forgive them for inflicting their language on us innocent Americans. They've got five stupid tenses, for God's sake! How French kids learn it is beyond me.

MONDAY, MAY 25TH

Peter texts to say he wishes he could be 100 percent certain he's gay.

I text back to say that the only certain things in life are death, finals, and the constant expansion of the universe, which was quite profound, I thought, and should put Peter's sexuality problems in perspective.

TUESDAY, MAY 26TH

7:30 A.M.: FINALS!!!!

Oh well, here we go. I touch the photo of Dad in the hallway and ask him to wish me luck before heading out the door and into the jaws of hell.

7:55 A.M.: HALLWAY, WAITING TO GO INTO GEOMETRY EXAM

Ollie told me that if you write on your skin, the ink goes into your bloodstream and travels to your brain. Obviously this is complete and utter bull, so why have I written about six hundred equations all over my arms, legs, and stomach?

9:45 A.M.: BACK OUT IN THE HALLWAY AFTER EXAM

Yes! One down, six million to go . . .

I think I did okay, but I felt a little weird toward the end — kind of light-headed. Maybe I have blood poisoning from all the BIC ink.

WEDNESDAY, MAY 27TH

1:15 P.M.: PHYSICS EXAM

Hannah Harrigan just ran out of the exam room crying. Is there a law against distracting people during exams? There damn well should be. I had to start question three all over again. I should report her to her policeman dad.

THURSDAY, MAY 28TH

Studying.

FRIDAY, MAY 29TH

3:30 P.M.: WALKING HOME WITH PETER, DAVEY, AND OLLIE AFTER ENGLISH WRITING EXAM

"Who'd you write your essay about?" asks Davey.

"I can't remember," I say.

"I wrote about my little brother," says Peter. "He's so cute. I'm sure Mrs. Barber will think it's adorable how he runs around with his diaper falling off and his wiener hanging out."

Delusional. Totally delusional.

"Come on, Josh," says Ollie. "Who'd you write about?"

I lie and say the mailman. It's a ridiculous thing to say, since I barely know our mailman let alone classify him as "someone who inspires happiness in my life," but I can't tell them I wrote about Ozzy.

I don't even think ferrets count as people . . . at least not if you're a stuck-up English Lit. teacher. She's probably a ferret hater. She might love wildlife and despise the way escaped ferrets are destroying our native small mammal populations.

Oh well, I guess I failed then. At least there's the literary analysis exam to make up for it in my final grade.

SATURDAY, MAY 30TH

10:00 A.M.: INNER SANCTUM

Studying.

11:00 A.M.

Taking a short break.

12:00 NOON

Still on a short break.

1:00 P.M.

Taking a long break.

1:10 P.M.

Working. I put the laundry in the washing machine,
ironed my shirt, did some dusting, matched some socks
(more or less), cut my toenails, scrubbed the toilet,
weighed myself, weighed Ozzy, and weighed my toenails.

Now that all that is done, I can settle down and study.

2:00 P.M.

God, I am so sick of studying.

SUNDAY, MAY 31ST

2:00 P.M.: KITCHEN

I ask my sister if she will test me on some French, and
miraculously she agrees.

2:05 P.M.

I have a huge argument with my sister about the
importance of *un* and *une*. My sister says I have to get
them right or I will fail my exam miserably.

I say, "Well, I bet you didn't get them right."

She says, "No, and I failed miserably, didn't I? You
stupid jerk."

MONDAY, JUNE 1ST

3:15 P.M.: WALKING HOME WITH OLLIE

Today was French and chemistry. They both went okay, but Ollie is worried about world history. He couldn't remember the first thing about the Russian Revolution, so he wrote an essay on sandwiches.

"It'll get me a few points, don't you think?" he asks.

"Definitely," I lie.

TUESDAY, JUNE 2ND

4:00 P.M.: INNER SANCTUM

I take a break from studying to practice some guitar. Just because the Jackson was bought doesn't mean I'm going to give up my dream of becoming a famous metal guitarist. Anyway, I can now play the pentatonic scale in all five positions in under twenty seconds. I bet even Kirk Hammett would struggle to do that — at least on a pathetic nylon-string for eight-year-olds.

WEDNESDAY, JUNE 3RD

8:50 A.M.: HALLWAY WAITING FOR ENGLISH LITERATURE EXAM TO START

I'm standing there pondering why we have to have

two English exams — I mean, if you can write, you can surely read — when Ollie rushes up to me and says, "You know the book *To Kill a Mockingbird*?"

"Well, yes," I say. "We have been studying it for the past six months."

"Right," says Ollie. "So what actually happens?"

I try to condense the entire plot of *To Kill a Mockingbird* into five minutes. I have never had such an intrigued audience. About twenty people are hanging on my every word as I go through the book's various themes, characters, language, and style. If the Metal God thing doesn't work out, I might have to become an English teacher.

FML.

THURSDAY, JUNE 4TH —
ONE MONTH TILL MY BIRTHDAY!

In thirty days' time, I'll be seventeen. Jesus, I'm getting old!

I hope I don't have a mid-teen crisis like Davey.

FRIDAY, JUNE 5TH

Message from Peter @PeterTheTweeter11: *Why not take a break from studying and follow me on Twitter?*

Message from me: *I'd rather be studying.*

SATURDAY, JUNE 6TH

Next week I have exams every day so it's solid studying. Catch you on the flip side . . .

SIX DAYS LATER: FRIDAY, JUNE 12TH

3:20 P.M.: WALKING HOME FROM SCHOOL

Yes, I made it! I managed to get through all my exams this week without:

1. **Running down the hallway screaming**

2. **Throwing my pens across the room and storming out**

3. **Getting kicked out for whispering**

4. **Getting kicked out for looking up answers on my cell phone**

5. **Getting kicked out for consulting notes that I stuffed into my underwear**

All of these things happened to one or another of my peers.

SATURDAY, JUNE 13TH

2:00 P.M.: PARK. ONLY TWO EXAMS TO GO!

I meet Davey in the park so we can take our minds off exams for a while.

"How's the therapy going?" I ask.

"Okay," says Davey. "My therapist says that my self-esteem is improving all the time. I can even bump into inanimate objects like doors now without apologizing to them."

"Well, that's great, Davey!" I say.

"I've also realized that being thin is not the answer," says Davey.

I feel like saying, *The answer to what? What is it not the answer to?* But it's probably best if we don't get into anything too deep/depressing, so I just ask if his therapist is hot.

"Not really," says Davey. "She's about sixty and has stubby gray hairs sticking out of her chin."

"Not exactly fantasy material then." I laugh.

"Funny you should say that . . ." begins Davey.

"Studying, Davey!" I say, jumping up quickly. "We can't put it off any longer!"

SUNDAY, JUNE 14TH

4:00 P.M.: INNER SANCTUM

Peter texts saying not to bother studying seismology, because it never comes up on the earth science exam.

Thanks, Peter. You could have told me that before I spent the last three hours drilling seismic waves, plate tectonics, and the results of the 1906 San Francisco earthquake into my poor overworked, undernourished brain.

TUESDAY, JUNE 16TH

9:45 A.M.: EARTH SCIENCE EXAM

Yes! A question on the San Francisco earthquake! In your face, Peter!

I'm getting into the swing of exams now. It's a shame there's only one left.

THURSDAY, JUNE 18TH

2:00 P.M.: LAST EXAM — SOCIAL STUDIES

I just wrote a pretty impressive essay on the moral issues surrounding animal testing. I said that all animal testing should be banned — especially testing on ferrets.

Instead I argued that scientists should test on lowlifes who beat up old ladies. I hope this isn't too offensive. If Mr. Higginbotham was once a lowlife who beat up old ladies, I'm screwed.

Anyway, the nightmare is over! Thank God!

At least final exams are.

Life in general goes on, of course.

7:30 P.M.: OLLIE'S HOUSE

Tonight we're having a sleepover at Ollie's house to celebrate finishing our finals. His parents had to go to a funeral up north and won't be back till tomorrow. Generally, Mrs. Hargreaves only lets Ollie have a couple of friends over at a time (which is one more than my mom!), but tonight there will be four of us — Ollie, Davey, Peter, and me.

I arrive late because Mom made me drop a bunch of magazines off at Mrs. Stokes's.

This should only have taken ten seconds, but Mrs. Stokes insisted that I come in so that she can see how tall I've grown and quiz me about school. Why are old people so interested in school? It must be because they forget how awful it was.

Anyway, Davey and Peter are already there (at Ollie's, not Mrs. Stokes's), and they have virtually demolished the smoky bacon chips, which is annoying since those are my favorite.

We do some Facebook stalking and then decide to watch the three *Lord of the Rings* movies back to back. It's quite a challenge, but Ollie has ordered tons of pizza, so we feel up to it. We settle down with our food and prepare to be transported to the vales of the Shire.

"Um," says Peter after Bilbo has disappeared dramatically from the festivities and Gandalf has hit his head on Bilbo's ceiling light (very uncool for a wizard). "Anyone wanna watch something a little less hobbity?"

Well naturally, I'm a big LOTR fan . . . but it does lack a certain something. Boobs, to be exact. Not that this would worry Peter.

"Fine by me," I say. "What have you got, Ollie?"

"What haven't I got," says Ollie. He hands over a stack of what look like photo albums, but they turn out to be full of DVDs. His parents belong to this club where you order DVDs, copy them, and send them back, so Ollie has more movies than all of Netflix.

"As long as it's got action, violence, and swearing, I'm good," I say after ten minutes or so of flipping through the books. "A little bit of female nudity wouldn't hurt, but I can live without it."

"Can you?" says Ollie.

"For the time being," I say.

"How do you feel about drug use?" says Ollie.

"I'm cool with that," I say.

"Mom won't let me watch anything with drugs in it," Peter says.

"Okay, no drugs. Horror?"

"I'd rather not," says Peter. "I don't like to see people suffering."

"What? Peter, you're weird! Okay, what do you want to watch?" I ask.

"How about this?" Peter says, holding a copy of *Up*.

"No!" I say, probably too quickly. "Um, me . . . no wait, my mom and Maddie went to see that, and they said it wasn't very good."

"I heard it was great," says Peter.

"Overrated, they said," I say.

"Well," says Ollie, closing the final album. "That's it. Over a hundred movies, and we can't decide on a single one to watch. Of course, there are . . ." Ollie grins sheepishly. "No . . . better not."

"What?" we say.

"Um, well . . . there are some DVDs on top of my parents' bookshelf. I don't think I'm supposed to know about them though."

"Really?" I say. "What are they?"

"Well, the thing is, they're at the back, and I can't quite reach —"

"Ollie," I say. "Have you never considered getting a chair?"

Ollie looks embarrassed, which is rare for him. "The thing is, I'm worried Dad'll find out."

"The only way that'll happen is if you leave the

DVD in the player," I say. "And no one would be stupid enough to do that!"

We get a chair from the office and wheel it into Ollie's parents' room. Since I am the tallest, I am chosen to risk life and limb on the swiveling thing. It's a stretch, but I manage to grab a couple from the dusty depths. They are all copies so they don't have pictures, but the titles have been written on in marker.

"*Yoga for the Over-Forties*," I say. "Hmm, that doesn't sound too good . . . *Painting in Oils — Unleashing the Creative You!*" I look down and say, "Are you pranking us, Ollie?"

"Reach farther back," he urges.

"Okay hold on, what's this? *Confessions of a Stay-At-Home Mom*. Ah, now we're getting somewhere."

I go up on my tiptoes and reach back farther.

"*Angie Gets Her Fill. Bonkers in Sweden. Lust of the LESBIAN LOVE NEST!*"

I notice Ollie looks kind of uncomfortable.

"What's up?" I say.

"It's just . . . well, it seems kinda wrong . . ."

"Okay," I say. "Let's just watch this one. *Big Bertha*. It sounds like a comedy more than anything."

I put everything back just like I found it, and we take *Big Bertha* downstairs.

Ollie gets up and turns off the TV.

"Jeez!" I say.

"Holy crap!" says Ollie.

"That Bertha made Megan Fox look like a dude!" says Davey.

"Are you okay, Peter?" I say. "You're not like . . . traumatized or anything?"

"No, I am just so happy!" cries Peter, jumping up from the sofa.

"What?" we all say. "Why?"

"Because I'm finally 100 percent certain I'm gay!" he says.

SATURDAY, JUNE 20TH

Ollie is grounded — his dad found *Big Bertha* in the DVD player. Luckily, my mom knows nothing about it, and I don't think Mr. and Mrs. Hargreaves are going to tell her.

Jeez, I will never look at Mr. Hargreaves the same way again. He seemed like such a nice, quiet man. The sort of man who'd enjoy puttering around with his tomato plants, waxing his car — that sort of thing. It's hard to believe he's a raving sex maniac.

SUNDAY, JUNE 21ST

11:00 A.M.

It's the Junior Prom on Friday. Not that I'll be going, since I have nothing to wear . . .

11:05 A.M.

I'm a genius! I just thought of the best excuse! I quickly text my friends.

11:10 A.M.: KITCHEN

Davey just texted back to say I have to go because there will be free food at the dance.

Ollie just texted back to say I have to go because there will be free booze at the parties afterward.

Peter just texted back to say I have to go because he's gonna come out!

Guess I'd better find something to wear then.

MONDAY, JUNE 22ND

5:00 P.M.: INNER SANCTUM

Mom gets me to try on Dad's old suit for the Junior Prom, but the jacket is way too big. "You're not as broad shouldered as your . . ." she starts to say.

I say, "I know — it's not fair. Why couldn't I have inherited Dad's muscles?"

Mom takes a deep breath, looks like she's about to say something, and then dashes out into the hallway.

"Uh, Mom," I call. "I'm sorry. I didn't mean to upset . . ."

But she's already in her room, and the door's shut.

TUESDAY, JUNE 23RD

Message from Peter @PeterTheTweeter11: *Hurry — the next person to follow me will receive a free bag of smoky bacon chips!*

Message from me: *Oh, all right.*

WEDNESDAY, JUNE 24TH

3:00 P.M.: MRS. STOKES'S HOUSE

With great reluctance and a sick feeling in my stomach, I try on Mrs. Stokes's husband's suit. Mr. Stokes has been dead for fifteen years, and for all I know, he could've died in this very suit. It certainly smells that way.

Anyway, thankfully, the sleeves are way too short. Mom almost yanks them out at the seams trying to make them long enough, but it's no use.

"Damn," she says, looking at my arms accusingly.

"What a shame," says Mrs. Stokes. "You look just like my Albert, God rest his soul."

I shake my head as I remove the jacket. "It is a shame," I say. "The suit is great. I would've loved to have worn it."

Mom grabs my arm and ushers me to the door. "Don't push your luck," she growls.

THURSDAY, JUNE 25TH

10:00 A.M.: SUIT-ABLE ATTIRE FASHION RENTAL SHOP WITH MOM AND NANA

"We want a nice, cheap suit," Mom explains to the shopkeeper, whose name is Madge.

"Ah," says Madge. "Which of those two criteria is the most important? Nice or cheap?"

"Cheap," says my mom.

I spend the next twenty minutes heaving myself into various suits, all of which make me look like . . . yep, a complete moron.

"Well, now this one is a little more pricey," says Madge. "But with suits, you know, you get what you pay for."

"Go ahead," moans Mom. "You might as well try it."

I retreat once more into the curtained closet, struggle into the suit, and emerge blinking in the light.

"Now that is a nice suit," says Nana, "very Clark Gable."

Who the hell is Clark Gable?

"Oh yes," agrees Madge. "Or . . . now who is it you remind me of? I know! Bruce Willis. You know, back in his *Moonlighting* days."

Bruce Willis?

But he's bald, isn't he?

And about fifty?

Good-looking though, I guess. Certainly a babe magnet.

"We'll take it," I say.

7:00 P.M.: INNER SANCTUM

Ozzy is sleeping on the suit! Every inch of fabric is smothered in his coarse white and black hairs.

Great. I will now look more like a giant ferret than Bruce Willis. Why, Ozzy? Why?

8:00 P.M.

Picking hairs off the suit.

11:00 P.M.

Still picking hairs off the suit. Only about six hundred million billion to go . . .

FRIDAY, JUNE 26TH

7:45 P.M.: THE JUNIOR PROM!

This Junior Prom thing is completely over the top. People are going in stretch limos, for God's sake. Needless to say, I have to walk, but at least there are a few of us, so we're less likely to get yelled at, egged, or spat on from a car.

I've met up with Ollie, Peter, and Davey. Ollie should still be grounded, but his mom spent a "small fortune" on his suit, so he's allowed to go.

Peter shows me the button he's wearing which says "100% gay and proud." I give him a high five.

We arrive at the Lofty Oaks Hotel, and I must say — it looks very upscale.

"Four stars," says Davey, looking up at the sign. "Not bad."

I don't tell Davey that the only hotel I've stayed in was rated two stars, and one of those stars looked like it had been drawn on in marker.

Inside, there's an area for dancing, some tables with food, and a small stage with a weird-looking band. There are girls in long ball gowns everywhere. They look very different from when they are in their school clothes. Some of them are almost looking attractive.

"Let's get some food before it's all gone," says Ollie.

This sounds like a plan, so we head over to the food tables.

"Oh look, it's the three musky queers," says Lydia.

Great, it's Lydia, Hannah, and Becky — my least favorite people.

"Actually," I say, with what I hope sounds like sarcasm, "there's four of us. That math exam must've been tough for you, huh, Lydia?"

"Did someone say something?" she says, looking around at everyone except me. "Oh no — my mistake."

I decide not to take the bait, partly because I have just said something vaguely witty, and partly because Davey beats me to it.

"You know, for a skinny person, you are really full of yourself," he says.

Phew! This is a barbed insult coming from Davey. Clearly the therapy sessions have paid off! Anyway, Lydia looks kind of stunned.

"Well, I might be slim," she says grabbing an extra slice of pizza. "But at least I can put on weight. You'll always be ugly."

God, what a jerk. "No, he won't," I snap back. "He's getting his nose done as soon as he starts making money, so there!"

"Shh!" whispers Davey. "Alert the whole damn school, why don't you?"

I must admit, things did get kind of quiet. Quite a few people are looking at Davey — particularly at his nose.

"There's no shame in getting cosmetic surgery," I tell him. "Everyone does it. People even get their dicks done."

"Really?" says Peter.

"Yes," say. "They get them lengthened."

"Well, I didn't think anyone would get it shortened!" says Peter, snorting happily.

I grab a few sandwiches and the last remaining deviled egg and pour myself some soda — might as well get something out of this sham of an evening.

"So, um, how much does it cost?" asks Peter, hustling closer and causing me to spill some soda on my sandwiches and drop my egg.

"I don't know," I tell him. God, Peter is a pain sometimes. "Where the hell did that egg go?"

"Were you thinking of getting it done?"

"No!" I tell him. "Why would you think that?"

"It's just — you seem to know a lot about it."

"Look, I am not an expert on dick extensions! My dick is a perfectly normal 5.7 inches, thank you very much!"

Suddenly everyone around me goes quiet again. A few people are giggling into their bruschetta. Lydia gives me a disgusted look.

Oh God, 5.7 inches . . . that's probably really small!

"Unextended, that is," I say. "Extended it's . . . oh I don't know, like two feet . . ."

Okay, there is no hope now. I have exposed myself as a complete perv with a grotesquely massive dick. Awesome. I might as well go home and flog myself with a broken bottle.

Except that . . . well, I think I see Becky Calbag smile at me. Is it a smile? It looks like one.

Nah, it's probably just a sneer gone wrong.

SATURDAY, JUNE 27TH

9:00 A.M.: INNER SANCTUM

So, I didn't hook up with anyone, I didn't get drunk, my deviled egg was never recovered, everyone thinks I have a penis deformity, and Davey isn't speaking to me. Other than that, the Junior Prom thing went pretty well.

One week till my birthday!

MONDAY, JUNE 29TH

11:00 A.M.: INNER SANCTUM

Davey is speaking to me again — but only because he wants to show off his new Xbox guitar game. Lucky for him, I am a very good friend, so I agree to go over and be hideously humiliated.

Also, I am bored out of my mind.

Also, I want to make sure he's getting me a present for my birthday — five days to go!

WEDNESDAY, JULY 1ST

Three days to go.

THURSDAY, JULY 2ND

Two!

FRIDAY, JULY 3RD

It's my birthday tomorrow (and the Fourth of July, but I prefer to keep the attention focused on my birthday). I will be seventeen. I check eagerly under the bed for my leather-bound notebook.

Have I achieved a single one of the things I wanted to achieve before reaching seventeen?

No.

SATURDAY, JULY 4TH — MY 17TH BIRTHDAY!

9:30 A.M.: KITCHEN

It wasn't a sneer gone wrong, it was a smile! I know this because Becky sent me a card for my birthday. It has a ferret on the front that looks a lot like Ozzy. She signed it *Love, Becky XO*. Not "best wishes" or "from," but "love!" And a kiss too!

Speaking of kisses, Aunt Sarah sent me three. Mrs. Stokes four. Peter six (kind of worrying), and Mom a whole bunch, plus she wrote, *To my wonderful boy*. It's too bad she isn't as nice in real life as she is in her cards.

Anyway, the important thing is that I have a card from a girl — a girl who likes ferrets. It's true that before today I couldn't stand Becky, but that was because she hung out with Lydia. You can't judge a person solely by their friends! Also, I kinda thought she hated my guts, but maybe Mom's right that I'm a little paranoid. From now on, I'm gonna try to be a lot more positive about stuff.

I open the remainder of my cards. Nana sent me one with flashing text on the front that says "Hooray! You are 12!" Her memory must be acting up again. She did remember to put thirty bucks in though, which is pretty awesome.

Davey made me a card that is a montage of metal superheroes. He has included a few people who aren't metal, such as Jon Bon Jovi and Freddie Mercury, but this is a common mistake among the uninitiated.

Ollie drew an excellent and highly pornographic Big Bertha on his. It's very funny, but probably not one for the mantel.

"Here you go, bro," says my sister, giving me a smile. "Knock yourself out. It's fifty bucks. I've been saving up my tips forever, so don't go wasting it on metal crap."

I find that my allergies are acting up and have to quickly wipe my eyes on my sleeve.

"Thanks, sis," I say.

"Well," says Mom. "Lots of money for you to spend on our shopping trip."

Usually I hate shopping, but that's because the only things I ever get are shoes and underwear and the occasional "tasteful" T-shirt that isn't in any way cool. You might think that there's no such thing as an uncool T-shirt, but believe me — Mom manages to find them and buy them in bulk.

I will put up with all this today, however, because I now have eighty bucks, and while obviously some must go toward an electric guitar, I'm going to treat myself for once and spend some of it on CDs!

"We'll visit Ned on the way back from town," Mom goes on.

"Ned?" I say.

"Mr. Pitman," says Mom.

"What?" I groan. "But it's my birthday. You said you'd take the day off."

"This isn't work, Josh. Ned wants to see you."

"Why?" I say.

"Well, he wants to wish you a happy birthday," she says. "You know how he likes to give you a little something on your birthday."

Yeah, little something is right. Last year he gave me a pack of playing cards with breeds of dogs on the back. Everyone knows I'm a ferret person. The year before, it was a stress ball he'd gotten for free with the *Times*. To be fair, that's been pretty useful, though.

3:00 P.M.: DOWNTOWN, MORRIS CAFÉ

Finally, Mom has agreed we can stop for lunch.

"Have whatever you want," she says. "Don't worry about the price."

This is not quite as generous as it seems given that nothing on the Morris menu is exactly Bobby Flay, but it's nice to have something other than a cheese sandwich for a change.

I ask for a burger and fries with salad on the side, followed by chocolate lava cake. Mom's eyes look startled for a few seconds, but she manages to suppress her phobia of spending money and nod her agreement.

Once we're sitting down, I toy with the idea of taking out my recently purchased CDs, but one has a lot of blood and dismembered bodies on the front, which might upset some of the other diners. I'll have to wait till we get home. I can't wait to show them to Ollie and the others.

"So can Ollie, Davey, and Peter come over this evening?" I ask through a mouthful of salad.

"Well, we're going to see Ned. Remember?" says Mom.

"Yes, but we won't be there all evening, will we?"

Mom stirs her coffee. "You see your friends almost every day," she tells me. "You can invite them over tomorrow."

I'd like to argue and point out that today is my birthday, but it's probably not worth the hassle, especially since Mom has been fairly nice to me, and I'm trying to be more positive and stuff. Besides, I don't want my burger to get cold.

6:00 P.M.: NED'S (A.K.A. MR. PITMAN'S)

Ned's house is like an oven on a high setting, so I offer to take Minty out for a quick walk around the block, but Mom says there's plenty of time for that and asks me to sit on the sofa. She gives me a brief, odd-looking smile before sitting down herself.

"Well, happy birthday, son," says Ned.

"Thanks," I say.

"Here you go. Here's a little something from me."

Ned hands over what turns out to be a pack of plastic guitar picks. Wow, this is actually a pretty useful present. There are six different ones, all different thicknesses and colors. If I'd have been a girl, I'd have probably really liked them. In fact, I do really like them.

I line them up in order of ascending thickness. The smallest one is like a sheet of paper (0.3 millimeters, pale blue). The thickest (1.3 millimeters, orange) is a real hardcore pick. You could poke someone's eyes out with this sucker.

"Thanks," I say. "They're really nice."

"Of course they won't be much use for that kids' nylon-string you've got, will they?" says Ned.

"Um?" I say.

With a tremendous effort, he gets up from his chair, hobbles to the corner of the room, and brings out something cocooned in old Christmas paper. It's big and kind of . . . kind of guitar shaped!

For a second I have what Mom would call a hot flash. My heart starts thudding, and my breaths come short and shallow.

It can't be the Jackson, can it? Can it? Eagerly, I rip off the paper . . .

It isn't.

I should have known that the wondrous Jackson would never be mine. It is, however, a guitar, and although it's not V-shaped, it is an interesting shape — kind of like a dagger.

It's green, and the make is ProStar UltraSmooth,

which sounds kind of like a deluxe brand of condom, but so what! It's an electric guitar, and it's mine!

"Thanks!" I say. "Wow, this is amazing!"

"Your mom told me you were saving up for one," says Ned. "I hope you don't mind that it's secondhand?"

"Not at all," I say. "It's awesome."

"Anyway, if it works out okay for you," says Ned, "I'll take out some of my savings and get you the Jackson your mom says you want. Like the one that was in Steve's Emporium, right?"

"Huh? Oh no, you don't have to do that," I say, astonished. "Someone else bought it already, and anyway it was really expensive. I mean really . . ."

"It's the least I can do," says Ned. "For my own flesh and blood . . ."

"Um, what . . . ?" I say. I look at Mom, who is leaning forward on the sofa, hands clenched and looking like she's about to throw up.

"I'm sorry, Josh," she says, laying a hand on my knee. "I should've told you this a long time ago."

"Told me what?" I say, edging away.

"Uh . . ."

"Mom?"

My mom clears her throat. "Ned is your, um . . ."

I grab the guitar and run for the door.

6:50 P.M.: SOME RANDOM STREETS

I walk around the streets for a while, gazing in people's windows at their flickering TV screens, but then it starts to rain, and I am forced to take cover in the grocery store. I kind of look like a dick, wandering around the refrigerators with a green dagger-shaped guitar under my arm, but what's new?

I note that frozen peas are on sale and that a twin pack of pepperoni pizzas works out to be a dollar cheaper than buying the same pizzas individually. I don't really like pepperoni though; someone once told me it was donkey meat.

The lady working at the register looks pissed off, and I realize that she's trying to close the store for the night, so I am forced out in the rain again.

I'm not sure what to do next. I consider going to Davey's, but Davey seems a lot happier since he's started therapy, and I don't want to be a downer. Ollie is a good friend, but he's about as understanding as a chicken potpie. And Peter? Well, Peter is too understanding. I can't cope with his over-the-top sympathy right now.

What I'd really like to do is go to Finland and join a metal band, but I have no money and no idea which plane to catch.

I am seventeen years old, and I don't have a clue who I am.

I thought I knew where I came from
It guided the way like a flame
But now it is raining inside me
And darkness is all that remains

From the album: *Raining Inside Me,*
by Josh Walker

SUNDAY, JULY 5TH

6:00 P.M.: INNER SANCTUM

It's the day after my birthday, and it's the worst day of my life. I am lying on my bed, staring at the ceiling, and trying very hard to make sense of things. It wouldn't have been so bad if I'd been the love child of a mad, passionate affair with an international rock star, but no — I was the unintended outcome of a fling with an elderly plumber. My mom has been very quiet. I think she's trying to stay out of my way for a while, which is fine by me.

There's a knock at the door, and my sister appears. Seeing her only adds insult to injury because my sister, you see, is not the offspring of Ned.

Suddenly the mystery of why she is so much more attractive than I am becomes clear — she had a different dad! A cooler, tanner, more handsome dad whose photo still hangs in the downstairs hallway and probably will forever unless I can somehow get Ozzy to smash it.

She sits down on the bed and puts her arm around my shoulder. "You okay?" she says.

Oh yeah, just peachy.

"I'm okay," I say.

"Try not to be too hard on Mom."

Hah! Easy for you to say. Mom has been hard on me since the day I was born!

"Humph," I say.

"If it's any consolation," she says, "Mom only told me the day before your birthday. I don't even think Mr. Pitman knew until very recently."

Oh, that's okay then!

"Well, if you wanna come down for a snack, I made some ants on a log."

My sister says this with a glint in her eye, as if I'm gonna leap up and cry, "Wow, ants on a log. Thanks, sis! Why am I worrying about having lived a lie for the past seventeen years when I could be downstairs eating ants on a log?"

"Awesome," I say.

She smiles and turns to open the door.

"But he's so old," I blurt out.

"Mr. Pitman? He's not that old. Fifty-six, I think Mom said."

"He looks about seventy."

"Well, that's the arthritis . . ."

"Also," I say. "Also. Why did Mom have to wait until now to tell me? Why not tell me when I was like, six or seven or ten? Why ruin a perfectly decent birthday?"

"Maybe she thought you would understand better when you were older," she says.

"Wrong!" I say.

"The thing is, Josh," says my sister. "It won't seem like it now, but actually, you are lucky. You have a dad who you can spend time with and get to know. I'll never be able to do that. When you think about it, it's probably the best birthday present Mom could've given you."

I don't even bother answering that.

"He used to be in a glam rock band, you know," she goes on. "Nimble-Fingered Ned, they called him. That guitar he gave you was his."

The door softly clicks shut behind her, and I hear her footsteps going down the stairs. Glam rock! Typical!

I grab the glam rock guitar and look it over. It's not in bad condition. There are a few chips on the body, but it gives it a kinda used and abused look, which is all right. Also, it's cut away, which makes it easy to reach the higher frets. Speaking of which, I count them out and find that there are twenty-two.

8:00 P.M.

It has taken me two hours, but I have more or less

mastered "One" by Metallica. Ozzy seems to like it. He was dancing along in his cage and making lots of dooking noises. Of course, it'll sound even more awesome when I eventually get an amp and can blast the roof off this shithole.

Anyway, I'm thinking that if I can play this, then maybe I really can be a metal guitarist one day. Whatever happens, I still have that.

8:10 P.M.: PASSAGE TO FORBIDDING GATEWAY

At the bottom of the stairs, I do a double take. There are now two pictures on the wall: my dad — or actually, my sister's dad — and Ned.

Ned looks about thirty years old. He has long, curly hair, thick black eyeliner on, and pants that look so tight, they seem stuck to his legs!

Mom comes up and looks at the picture with me. "Can I talk to you for a moment?" she asks.

I shrug and follow her into the living room where we sit in opposite chairs.

"I owe you an explanation," she says.

"Yep," I say.

Mom proceeds to explain how seventeen years and nine months ago, Ned came over to fix the washing machine — yes, seriously! Anyway, he got to telling Mom how his wife was cheating on him and didn't love him anymore. How you go from talking about a blocked drain to marital problems, I don't know, but they managed it.

Anyway, Mom was sympathetic, and, being lonely herself, she invited Ned to stay for dinner. Ned was so appreciative that he went out and bought a nice, expensive bottle of wine, and one thing led to . . .

"Oh my God," I say. "You got trashed! That's why you won't let me drink!"

Mom looks down at her lap and nods.

"And not content with just that," I say, "not content with just that, you had sex with a married man, got pregnant, and lied to everyone about who the real father was!"

"I did tell Nana," she says. "And I would have told Maddie's dad too . . ."

"Except he went and died!" I blast back.

Mom is dabbing at her eyes now. "It was just that once," she says. "Just a silly mistake. By the time I realized I was pregnant, Ned had made up with his wife, and they seemed so happy together . . . well, anyway, I decided to keep it a secret. I think a few people might have suspected, but no one could prove anything. Not even Shirley Heppinstall, though she certainly tried hard enough."

"Clint's mother?" I say.

Mom blows her nose. "Yes."

"Hmm," I say, remembering what Clint had said in the restaurant about my family not being all that innocent.

"So," I go on, "I'm guessing you decided to come clean to Mr. Pitman — I mean Ned — after his wife went off with that delivery dude."

Mom nods. "I noticed how well you two were getting along, and I thought you both deserved to know. Ned was delighted — he's always wanted children — but I know it's been . . . harder for you."

I don't say anything.

"Anyway," says Mom, reaching below the chair. "I thought you might like to see this."

Mom pulls out her leather-bound notebook — the same one I found a few months ago in her dresser drawer.

Now I know what her secret was!

She opens it up near the middle to the eighties band photos I saw before.

"He was an excellent guitarist," she says, passing me the book. "You must get your musical talent from him."

Mom is quiet while I look at the pictures of Ned and his band.

Then, when I pass the book back to her, she says, "I'm so sorry, Josh. Can you forgive me?"

I don't know.

MONDAY, JULY 6TH

7:30 A.M.: INNER SANCTUM

It's been another sleepless night, and I am lying on my bed staring at the ceiling. I seem to be doing a lot of this lately.

I feel sad that I didn't know Ned when I was growing up and before his arthritis got so bad. We could've gone to shows together. He could've taught me to play AC/DC solos from an early age. We might have even done weird stuff like play ball down at the park. All this makes me sad and angry. But . . .

I get that Mom was worried.

I get that we all make mistakes (admittedly, hers was a pretty big one). And, most of all, I get that she is really, really sorry and really, really upset — both things that are quite out of character for my mom. Especially the being sorry thing.

I also remember something my sister said . . .

"If you wanna come down for a snack, I made some ants on a log."

Nope, not that.

. . . "You have a dad who you can spend time with and get to know. When you think about it, it's probably the best birthday present Mom could've given you."

And I guess she's right. I guess it is better late than

never. Plus, it's kinda cool — in a slightly ironic way — to have an aging glam rocker as a dad!

I swing my legs off the bed and pull on some clothes.

If I do decide to forgive Mom, then it doesn't mean I'm gonna let her off easy . . .

7:45 A.M.: KITCHEN

"How are you feeling this morning, sweetie?" says Mom, pouring me a cup of coffee.

"I'm good," I say.

"Did you, uh, think any more about what I asked you yesterday?" she asks.

"I did, Mom," I say. "And I have decided that I can almost certainly forgive you. However, things are gonna have to change around here. And I mean seriously change."

"Like what?" says Mom, looking worried.

"Grab a seat," I say.

TUESDAY, JULY 7TH

2:00 P.M.: CURL UP AND DYE

"For f***'s sake, sit still," says my sister. "Do you wanna be stabbed in the eye?"

"Let me think," I tell her.

"Don't talk!"

I am wondering if it's a good idea letting my sister pierce my ear. I am her first ever client, and she's even more nervous than I am.

"Wait," I say as she lunges at me with the stapler thing. "Are you absolutely sure this is not the gay ear?"

"Jesus! For the nine millionth time. Yes!"

"Okay, let's do it."

There's a jolt, a flash of pain, and then a feeling of relief that I can still breathe and see out of both eyes.

My sister stands back and looks at me critically.

"Wait," she says. "My left ear is actually your —"

"Huh?" I say.

"Nothing," says my sister quickly. "Nothing at all. Wow, looks great. It really suits you."

She shows me in a mirror, and it does look good. Yay, number 5 is crossed off the list!

WEDNESDAY, JULY 8TH

3:45 P.M.: SHOPPING WITH NED

I've been getting along really well with Ned — I mean Dad. Today we are shopping in Steve's Music Emporium for an amp!

"A fifty-watt one should be fine," says Ned, maneuvering his wheelchair around to get a better look. "Actually, fifty watts is going to sound pretty loud in your bedroom. It might even annoy your mom and sister a little."

"Cool," I say.

Ned grins and says, "Okay, let's start with this one."

I plug the Dagger of Death (as I now affectionately call my guitar) into a Peavey ValveKing, push the buttons up to ten, and launch into "Seek and Destroy" by Metallica. I manage to play for twenty seconds before Steve runs over and yanks out the plug.

THURSDAY, JULY 9TH

6:10 P.M.: KITCHEN

Yes! I am now the proud owner of a body piercing and a very loud amp! Plus, Mom just agreed that I can grow my hair out to my shoulders!

"You can always tie it back for interviews and things," says Mom, shaking out the dishcloth. "I've seen a few of those metal people with their hair pulled back, and it can look quite neat and respectable if it's washed and combed."

"Absolutely," I say. "Um, speaking of metal people, Mom, there's something I'd really like to do this Saturday."

"What's that?" says Mom.

FRIDAY, JULY 10TH

Text from Becky: *Yes I'd love to come. Thanks so much for inviting me XO*

Oh my God! Tomorrow is my first real date with a girl! An actual girl. Of the human variety.

And we aren't just going to the mall, or Starbucks, or even the train tracks. We are going to another country!

SATURDAY, JULY 11TH

4:00 P.M.: F.Y.E., TORONTO, CANADA

I feel kind of stupid getting Alexi Laiho to sign the Dagger of Death. Most people have CD covers or autograph books. No one has a guitar — let alone a giant green one — but it's too late now. I can't exactly hide it up my shirt. I look hopefully at Becky, but it's asking too much even of her ample frontage.

Becky and I are standing in a large record store in Toronto in a long line at the end of which sit Children of Bodom.

Yes, they are here. In the flesh! The concert tickets were all sold out, but at least we're catching their album signing.

I'm still amazed that Mom let me come. She even paid for it! I know she's worried we'll get lost or kidnapped or something, but she admits she's got to let me do more stuff. Plus all the worry will be worth it when I give her the locally made maple walnut fudge I bought for her, Ned, and Nana!

"Come on, Josh," says Becky.

A small gap has opened in front of me, and I rush to fill it, accidentally poking the headstock of my Dagger of Death up the backside of some giant of a metalhead in front. When he turns, he reveals a face partly covered in hair. He's like one of those Eastern moose you see up here, only not so intelligent looking.

"Sorry, dude," I say.

He gives me a "Go f*** yourself" stare, but doesn't look like he's about to gore me to death, so that's a bonus.

Several feet in front of me, some wiseass hands Janne (killer keyboardist) a bottle of Jack Daniels. Damn, all I have is a half-drunk bottle of Snapple and some Keebler cookies. Somehow I doubt they'll be received as eagerly. Why didn't I bring a present? At least I remembered to wear my Bodom T-shirt.

"You're next," says Becky excitedly.

I look up, and there's Alexi Laiho staring at me. "Hey there," he says. "Want me to sign that?"

I pass over the Dagger of Death.

"Cool guitar," he lies.

"Thanks," I say. "It's my dad's. He was in a rock band. Glam rock, unfortunately, but the genre did lay the groundwork for several sub-types of more hardcore . . ." Stop rambling, you idiot!

Alexi autographs the guitar, and then, just as I'm about to take it back, he starts to play a song on it! And not just any song but "Bed of Razorz," which is one of my all-time favorites!

"Nice tone," he says, handing back the Dagger of Death.

I feel kinda shaky, and a small boy behind is making things worse by kicking me in the ankle to get me to move forward.

"Get a f***ing move on!" someone down the line yells.

"Yeah, move it, you bastard!"

Reluctant but happy, I finally get myself together and manage to leave the store. Wow, how good was that!

We do some shopping for Becky, then head back to the bus station, clearing the crowds as we go with the majestic, newly signed Dagger of Death.

It's like a fifty-hour journey back on the bus, but it's been worth it.

"Can I ask you something?" I say once I carefully get the guitar stored in the overhead rack and collapse in my seat.

"Sure," says Becky.

"What is it you like about me exactly?"

"Well, you're nice," says Becky.

"Yeah?"

"Like that day in earth science when you opened all the windows to let that bee out."

"Oh yes," I say, remembering. "And everyone said I was a bee-loving moron."

Becky nods. "I'm a softie for animals too," she says. "Once I bought an overpriced brownie at the train station and gave half of it to a pigeon with only one foot."

"That sounds like me," I say. "Okay, kind to animals. Anything else?"

"And you're good at the guitar."

"Guitar Guru, yes."

"But mostly it's because you're weird," she says.

"I'm not weird," I say.

"Yes, you are," says Becky.

"Tell me one way that I'm weird," I say.

"Well, for a start, most of your Facebook friends are ferrets."

"Actually," I say, "Only half —" but before I can finish the sentence, Becky leans over and gives me a big kiss.

Yes! Number 1 on the list is achieved at last. I can't wait to get home and check it off in my leather-bound notebook.

About the Author

J. A. Buckle lives in Surrey, England and has two teenage children. In addition to writing, she designs websites, helps out at animal welfare charities, plays guitar, and takes her dog for walks.